"**The tractor's going** [
fuel pump soon," he
we can get by witho

"Good."

He straightened, turned to her and smiled. As his gaze locked on hers, his smiling expression drifted into serious waters. He reached up and brushed a strand of hair from her cheek.

"Oops. I got a little grease on you." He reached around his back, removed the rag he'd tucked into his pocket and dabbed it against her cheek.

Her lips parted at his gentle touch, and his movements stalled.

Her heart began to race. She knew where this was going and what would happen—if she'd let it.

Tell him no. Not here. Not now.

But this time, when he slipped his arms around her waist and drew her close, she shut out the voice of common sense. And when he lowered his mouth to hers, she didn't care about anything other than kissing him once more, even if it was for the very last time.

* * *

RANCHO ESPERANZA: Never lose hope for love

Dear Reader,

Last year, my personal hero and I traveled to Montana for the very first time. We flew into Kalispell and stayed with a friend in Big Fork. I loved that trip and decided that area would make a perfect setting for my new Harlequin Special Edition miniseries. Located just outside the fictitious town of Fairborn, Montana, Rancho Esperanza is a struggling and nearly bankrupt cattle ranch that's becoming a refuge for women in need of a place to live, heal and make a fresh start.

In *A Secret Between Us*, Callie Jamison is living at Rancho Esperanza and working as a waitress at the town diner, where she meets Ramon Cruz, a handsome younger man who has an alluring laugh, a warm smile and a muscular build.

Ramon is attracted to Callie, too, even when he learns that she's pregnant. But too much stands in their way—an age difference, his political aspirations, not to mention another secret Callie hasn't shared with him. Yet love often finds a way around obstacles that seem to be insurmountable.

I've enjoyed revisiting Montana in my memories while I wrote this first book. And book two, *Their Night to Remember*, will be out next month! So kick off your shoes, settle into your favorite reading spot and enjoy a trip to the quaint town of Fairborn—and to Rancho Esperanza.

Happy reading!

Judy

PS: I love hearing from my readers. You can contact me through my website, judyduarte.com, and you can find me at Facebook.com/judyduartenovelist.

A Secret
Between Us

JUDY DUARTE

HARLEQUIN

SPECIAL
EDITION

ISBN-13: 978-1-335-40468-8

A Secret Between Us

Harlequin Enterprises ULC
22 Adelaide St. West, 40th Floor
Toronto, Ontario M5H 4E3, Canada
www.Harlequin.com

Printed in U.S.A.

Recycling programs
for this product may
not exist in your area.

Since 2002, *USA TODAY* bestselling author **Judy Duarte** has written over forty books for Harlequin Special Edition, earned two RITA® Award nominations, won two Maggie Awards and received a National Readers' Choice Award. When she's not cooped up in her writing cave, she enjoys traveling with her husband and spending quality time with her grandchildren. You can learn more about Judy and her books on her website, judyduarte.com, or at Facebook.com/judyduartenovelist.

Books by Judy Duarte

Harlequin Special Edition

Rocking Chair Rodeo

Roping in the Cowgirl
The Bronc Rider's Baby
A Cowboy Family Christmas
The Soldier's Twin Surprise
The Lawman's Convenient Family

The Fortunes of Texas: Rambling Rose

The Mayor's Secret Fortune

The Fortunes of Texas: All Fortune's Children

Wed by Fortune

Brighton Valley Cowboys

The Boss, the Bride & the Baby
Having the Cowboy's Baby
The Cowboy's Double Trouble

Visit the Author Profile page
at Harlequin.com for more titles.

In memory of Betty Lou Astleford, who taught me how to be a daughter, sister, wife, mother and grandmother. I love you, Mom.

Chapter One

Callie Jamison's shift at the Meadowlark Café had been so hectic that she'd hardly had a chance to breathe, let alone check her text messages. Finally, an hour before she was to clock out, she took a quick break and walked out the front door.

Once outside, she sat on the oak-slatted wrought iron bench to the left of the restaurant's entrance and under the shade of a blue-and-white-striped awning. Then she withdrew her cell phone, an old flip-up model that made texting a real pain. But she couldn't complain. When she'd dropped her smartphone into a sink full of soapy water and dirty dishes back in March, she hadn't wanted to tap into her savings to replace it.

She flipped up the lid and took a look. Several texts had come in while she'd been at work. The most recent was from her doctor.

You have an appointment with Dr. Patel at our office tomorrow at 9:00 a.m.

Got it. She'd never forget that. She'd seen the nurse practitioner several weeks ago, but this would be her first visit to the doctor since moving to Montana, and she'd already asked for the day off. *Delete*. Next?

Don't forget to pick up Rascal from the groomers. They close at 4:30 today.

Admittedly, Callie's brain had been a little sluggish lately, but her friend Alana hadn't needed to remind her about the sweet Aussie cattle dog that Alana had inherited along with the Lazy M Ranch. Got it.

Callie had hoped to find yet another message waiting for her to read, and a wisp of disappointment fluttered through her. There was still no word from her son, Mikey. Not that she was worried. It's just that they'd always been close, and she felt a little lost when they went more than a day without any contact.

Mikey—or rather, Micah, as he preferred to be called now—was a brilliant premed student at Baylor with a keen interest in neuroscience. But unlike his other classmates, he had just turned sixteen.

Sixteen. Callie had barely been a year older than that when she'd given birth to him. She'd never forget the day the delivery room nurse first placed the squalling, red-faced infant in her arms, a newborn dependent upon a clueless teenage mom to take care of him when she could hardly take care of herself.

Her feeble attempts to nurse him left her feeling like a maternal failure, and she'd never felt so alone or out of her element. But enter a kindhearted nurse, a lactation consultant and a hospital social worker, and she'd managed to get by. With time, she became the kind of mother she'd never had, one who loved her child and always put him first.

In spite of her resolve to give Mikey the space he'd asked for and the trust and respect he deserved, now that he was at the university, she typed out a quick text to give him a little nudge. You doing okay? Then she pushed Send.

Before folding down the cell phone lid, she took a quick peek at the time—2:16. The café was nearly empty. The lunch crowd was gone, and early bird diners had yet to arrive, but she'd better go inside and get back to work. Mikey might have earned a full ride scholarship, but he still needed clothing and spending money. Her salary and tips barely gave her enough to cover both of their living expenses. And she wasn't about to tap into her savings unless she absolutely had to. She might not be able to build up her small nest egg these days, but she wasn't about to deplete it.

When approaching footsteps sounded, she glanced down the sidewalk to see Ramon Cruz, Fairborn's youngest council member, walking her way. Callie had only been in town for a few months and was just getting to know the locals, some of whom were nicer and more sociable than others. But it hadn't taken long for her to realize there was something special about Ramon.

His wife had left him a few months ago, and ever since then he'd been eating most of his meals at various restaurants in town—at least one of them at the Meadowlark Café. The couple's split had shocked the entire community, and almost everyone had been speculating about the reason. But Ramon had been so tight-lipped about the breakup that not even the gossipmongers had enough details to weave it into a juicy story.

"I didn't expect to see you out here," Ramon said. "You're usually inside, saving my favorite table for me."

Callie offered him a warm smile. "I've been working nonstop since seven this morning, so I was just taking a short break."

"I'm sure you earned it. I'm just glad you're still here."

So was she. And not just because Ramon was a good tipper. He seemed to always have a sparkle in his eyes and an easy grin that could brighten her day, especially the long, hard ones when all she wanted to do the moment she got home was to lie down and put her feet up. And that's just the kind of day she was having.

"When you didn't show up for lunch," she said, "I figured you'd decided to eat somewhere else today."

"What?" His lips quirked into a crooked grin. "And miss out on eating the best food in Fairborn, served by the friendliest face in Montana?"

"Always the charming politician," she said, a lighthearted tone in her voice. And one that came out a little too flirtatious for comfort. She'd have to try harder to tamp down her playful side whenever Ramon came around, although that wouldn't be easy. The tall, dark and gorgeous hunk with expressive brown eyes was one of the sexiest men she'd ever met. She'd never seen him shirtless, but broad shoulders and a muscular chest suggested he'd look impressive without one.

And Callie wasn't the only who found him attractive. Once word had gotten out that the hot young city councilman was unattached, the single women began approaching him like a band of wolves circling a chicken coop.

Callie couldn't blame them, though. Whether Ramon came to town wearing a flannel shirt, jeans and a cowboy hat or dressed to the hilt in a slick business suit, he definitely turned women's heads.

She got to her feet and stepped away from the bench. "It's time for me to get busy."

Ramon shot her a dazzling smile that nearly stole her breath away. Then he opened the café door and stood aside. "After you."

Their gazes momentarily locked, and she darn near froze in her tracks. She couldn't get over the amazing color of his eyes—a caramel brown with flecks of gold. Nor could she ignore his mountain fresh scent.

If he were a few years older, or if she were a few years younger…

Oh, for Pete's sake, Callie. Get a grip. She was clearly older than him. It was hard to say just how much, though. At least six or seven years, she suspected. Not to mention several other complications that made her attraction to him completely senseless. So she shook off any thoughts that were even remotely romantic.

Before stepping through the glass door he held open for her, she took one last glance at the display on her old-style cell and spotted a new message. *Oh good. That must be Mikey.*

She lifted an index finger to signal that she needed a moment. "I'll be right behind you, Ramon. I just need to answer this quickly."

"Sure. I'll see you inside."

Callie flipped the cell open, eager to make sure Mikey was doing well, that his college classmates were accepting him better than the kids at his high school had and that his dorky history professor had stopped referring to him as the boy genius.

She smiled in anticipation of Mikey's latest news as she checked her text, but the minute she spotted the sender's name, her stomach clenched and a wave of nausea rushed through her.

Dammit. Garrett Williamson. The lying jerk. She would've blocked his calls and texts if she'd thought he'd ever contact her again. And if her ancient phone actually had that function.

Hey! How's it going? Did you get things taken care of?

She studied the unsettling message, tempted to delete it without a response. But ignoring it would probably come back to haunt her in the long run.

She nearly typed out, *Lose my number.* Instead, she said, Yes—a simple response on a smartphone, but one that required nine thumb taps on a dumb one. Before sending her message, she made the required taps and added, No worries.

Not for Garrett, anyway.

She hit Send, then she slammed the phone shut. At least this time, she hadn't ended their conversation with him so angrily and abruptly that she'd drowned her phone!

Still, she continued to stand on the sidewalk, taking a moment to shake off her frustration and negativity, which wouldn't do her or the customers any good. As a bicyclist rode by, she drew in a deep, fortifying breath of fresh Montana air and slowly let it out.

At the city park across the way, a bit too close to the busy main drag for a mom's comfort, a couple of boys wearing matching red baseball caps played catch. If Callie hadn't needed to get back to work, she would've marched over to the kids who couldn't be more than seven or eight years old and suggested that they move back a bit, away from the street and closer to the playground.

At the sound of approaching footsteps and feminine chatter, Callie spotted Marianne Posey, one of the regulars, and another middle-aged woman heading toward the café, reminding her that she'd better go back to work. And back to the town councilman who had a way of lifting her mood and putting a smile on her face.

She took one last glance at the little boys and

decided that they seemed to know what they were doing. Mikey hadn't been the outdoorsy, playful type, so she didn't have any experience with youth sports. In fact, she didn't have much experience in anything besides kissing boo-boos, making study-time snacks, taking meal orders and refilling coffee cups. On the upside, she'd be using those boo-boo-kissing skills again in the near future.

Who would have guessed that after sending her son off to college she'd be pregnant again?

Ramon took a seat at a table near the window that provided a view of Elmwood Drive and the park across the street, where Jesse and Mark Johnson played catch. The brothers were on the Little League team Ramon coached, and he'd grown especially close to them over the past couple of weeks.

Jesse and Mark lived with Katie, their older sister, in a low-rent apartment complex on the edge of town and didn't get out this way very often. It was nice to see them practicing their skills during their free time. There were a lot of kids who'd rather spend their free time playing video games indoors.

Katie was probably cleaning the public restrooms at the park across the street, her part-time job with the city. Ramon had mentioned the opening to her in passing. He'd figured she might not be interested in taking on a chore like that, but she'd jumped at the chance and said, *I need the extra work.*

If the boys were still at the park when he finished his lunch, he'd go across the street and hit a few grounders and pop flies to them.

For now, he was ready for a hearty meal and a few laughs with his favorite waitress.

Callie Jamison was new in town, but in the few short months since she'd moved to Fairborn, she seemed to have fit right in. He'd even begun to think of her as one of the locals—and one he'd like to get to know a lot better.

She seemed to sense what her customers needed without being asked, whether it was salad dressing on the side, an extra napkin or a kind word and a smile. She even knew when someone wanted to be left alone, to eat their meal in peace and quiet.

Callie was attractive, too. Yet for some reason, Ramon got the feeling she didn't have any idea how pretty she was. Her work uniform—a scoop-neck white T-shirt with the Meadowlark Café logo on the shoulder, blue jeans and an apron—was no different than what the other two servers wore. But the other waitresses didn't have long, honey-brown hair, big blue eyes and a killer smile that made her stand out in a crowd. She seemed to actually like small-town life, and she didn't look down on the locals, no matter how they dressed or how they talked. Every time Ramon saw her smile or heard her laugh while serving the folks in the community, he wondered what it'd be like to spend time with her on one of her days off. And with each conversation they had, he found himself more and more tempted to ask her out. But he hadn't gotten that far. Not yet, anyway. His divorce wasn't final, although that was merely a formality, according to his ex.

Jillian had made it clear their marriage was over when she'd told him she refused to give up her dreams for his.

Living in Montana and being a local hero in this Podunk town might make you happy, she'd said, *but I'm miserable here, and you couldn't care less about how I feel.*

Ramon could have argued the point. He'd never wanted to see her unhappy. He'd loved her. But she'd been right. They'd wanted different things out of life. So he'd followed her out the door and watched as she drove away from the house with a rented U-Haul trailer hitched to the back of her car. He hadn't asked where she was going. He'd known. She'd loved New York City, where she would try to find work in the theater. That was her dream.

Disappointment tinged with sadness had draped over him as he watched her taillights disappear from sight, but those feelings weren't as heavy or burdensome as the realization that he'd failed to hold his marriage together.

He glanced out the window and spotted Callie standing on the sidewalk. She wasn't talking on her cell or even looking at it. Instead, she stared at the street with her fists planted firmly on her small waist, her back stiff, her shoulders tense. He could only see her profile, but worry was evident in her stance.

Not that it was any of his business, but one of the things he especially liked about her was her smile, and whenever he didn't see her wearing one, he felt compelled to toss a joke her way.

That's usually all it took to get her to laugh, a happy, mesmerizing sound that made a man glad to know he'd been the one to bring it out of her.

The café door squeaked open, drawing his attention away from the window, and Marianne Posey and Helena Davis entered. The two forty-something friends wearing black yoga pants and bright, oversize T-shirts—one neon pink, the other lime green—had clearly just come from the gym.

When Helena scanned the restaurant and her gaze landed on Ramon, her eyes widened, her cheeks flushed and she quickly turned toward the refrigerated case that displayed the desserts. He didn't doubt that the woman liked sweets, but she clearly meant to avoid him. And he supposed he couldn't blame her. She'd dated his dad for a while, and it hadn't ended well.

Helena had wanted a lot more out of the relationship than Ramon's father had, and they'd broken up. A month or two later, while having drinks with one of her friends, Helena had seen his dad walk in with another woman, and she'd had a public meltdown.

On the other hand, the moment Marianne spotted Ramon, she brightened and approached his table. "Hey, there! You're not eating alone, are you?"

Uh-oh. He sensed he was about to get some company and steeled himself.

"Rumor has it you've been spending a lot of time by yourself these days."

"No," he said, opting to change his plan rather than suffer with idle chitchat or hurt anyone's feelings. "I'm not eating alone. I'm ordering a sandwich to go. I've got to head back to city hall, so I'll just eat at the office." He nodded toward Helena, who'd remained near the entrance and studied a variety of desserts in the display case. "Are you ladies having a late lunch, too?"

Marianne laughed. "No, we ate earlier. We just came from the new fitness club down the street and thought we'd have a slice of pie before going home."

Ramon chuckled. "Sounds like a healthy choice to me."

"By the way," Marianne added, "my niece will be in town this weekend. She's moving to Fairborn in a couple of weeks and plans to work at the new hair salon. I thought it might be nice to have a little dinner party in her honor, and I'd love for you to come."

"A little dinner party" his butt. More like a setup.

"I can show you her picture," Marianne added.

"That's okay. I'm sure she's nice—and attractive. But I'm afraid I'll be tied up all weekend. Thanks for thinking about me, though."

"That's too bad." Instead of joining her friend, she studied him for a moment. "I hope you really do have other plans."

He cocked his head slightly, unsure where she was going with that.

She crossed her arms and shifted her weight to one foot. "That isn't just an excuse for you to stay home alone and wallow in your grief, is it?"

Why was she taking such an interest in his personal life? "Don't worry, Marianne. I've moved on. And I'm doing okay."

"I'm glad to hear that. You're a good man, Ramon." She scanned the restaurant until she found her friend heading toward a corner booth in the back of the restaurant. She nodded toward Helena. "I'd better go. But next time my niece is in town, I'll let you know."

Word of his single status had spread rapidly. Several of the girls he'd gone to high school with— actually, women in their mid- to late twenties now—as well as the curvy blonde barista who worked at the new coffee place near city hall had been coming on to him lately.

A lot of men in his boots might have jumped at the chance to add a little fun to their lives, but Ramon had been dragging his feet when it came to dating. Not because he was grieving Jillian's loss or harboring false hope. Hell, the day she left, they'd both known their split was inevitable. They hadn't even argued over who got what. The only thing either of them had really wanted was to be happy, which meant one of them would have to compromise their dreams and values, and that had been out of the question.

In some ways, he supposed they'd both won in the end. Too bad he couldn't savor the win when a good-size part of him felt like a failure.

The café door creaked open once again, and as Callie walked inside—not exactly smiling, but no longer looking as if she'd just been carjacked, Ramon's mood lifted.

As she walked toward the cash register, he studied her more carefully than he probably should, especially since the café was no longer empty. He couldn't help but wonder how long her golden brown hair would be if she didn't wear it pulled up in a neat topknot or woven in a tidy twist.

His gaze slipped down to her left hand, as it usually did each time he saw her, but a ring never appeared. And that didn't seem right. She was too pretty, too kindhearted not to have a fiancé or husband.

In spite of telling himself he wasn't interested in her, that it was too soon for any feelings to stir for another woman, he couldn't stop the questions from popping up in his mind. Was there a man in her life? Had there ever been?

She picked up a couple of menus from the stack they kept behind the register, then walked to his table.

"Do you need one of these?" she asked, her eyes crinkling at the corners.

He offered up a wink and a boyish grin. "Nope. I've pretty much got it memorized."

Aw. There it went. That sweet, dimpled smile that lit up her eyes and swept the worry from her face.

She lifted her pad and a stubby pencil from her apron pocket. "So, what'll it be?"

"I'll have the tri-tip sandwich and fries to go."

"You got it."

After placing his order with the cook, she crossed the restaurant to where Marianne and Helena now sat. The women must have mentioned that they'd come in for dessert, because Callie turned Marianne's menu over and pointed to the Sweets and Treats section on the back. They appeared to settle on something quickly, because Callie nodded, then headed for the display case.

Ramon glanced at his iPhone and checked his email. The mayor had just sent out the agenda for the next council meeting, including the new zoning ordinance that had upset several local businesses. That was expected, but Mayor Hawkins had neglected to add Ramon's proposal to fund a remodel of the old community center. So he fired off a reminder, adding his belief that the building might not be up to code and insisting that it be made a priority.

After serving Marianne and Helena two big slices of lemon meringue pie, Callie made her way back to Ramon with a large glass of iced tea. "I thought you might like something to drink while you're waiting for that sandwich."

Ramon didn't need to ask if it was sweetened. He'd only mentioned his preference once, and she always got it right. "Thanks."

She studied him for a moment, and her head tilted. "You seem a little lost in thought today."

He was, but not about politics or the town. He was tempted to ask her out. Was it too late to change his order, to ask to eat here after all?

As she turned toward the kitchen, he called her back to his table. "Callie, can I ask you a question?"

She glanced over her shoulder and blessed him with another pretty smile. "Sure. What is it?"

Before he could open his mouth, the sound of squealing tires echoed through the café as a car slammed on its brakes. He glanced outside to see Jesse Johnson lying on the street, his mitt and red baseball cap several feet away from his body, his brother, Mark, standing on the curb, stunned and gaping in disbelief.

Ramon's heart damn near dropped to the floor. He pushed his chair back, the legs scraping the tile floor, and, as he ran to the door, yelled, "Call 9-1-1!"

Chapter Two

Callie's stomach churned, and her heart pounded so hard that it throbbed in her ears. She grabbed the cell phone from her pocket and made the call.

"Dispatch," the operator said. "What's your emergency?"

"A child was hit by a car in front of the Meadowlark Café, and we need an ambulance right away." When the operator began to question Callie and ask for details, she pressed the phone against her ear and hurried outside to assess the situation better. "I'm not sure how old he is. About seven or eight, I think."

"Is he conscious?"

"Yes. He's crying. His nose is bleeding, and he's holding his head."

Gloria Reinhart, the Meadowlark Café's cook, must have overheard the commotion, because she ran out of the kitchen and hurried to the doorway. Both pie eaters, one of whom carried her plate and fork, did the same.

"What's going on?" Gloria asked.

"A little boy was hit by a car," one of the pie eaters said.

"I think he's one of Katie Johnson's kids." Gloria clicked her tongue and slowly shook her head. "I've always thought she should watch them closer."

Gloria was a good cook, but she had a tendency to be harsh and judgmental. Callie didn't challenge her often, but she couldn't let that unfair assumption go by without comment. "Sometimes accidents happen, no matter how closely a mother watches her children."

Ramon knelt beside the injured boy he called Jesse, talking to the child, reassuring him. Several other people had already gathered around them, including the driver, an older gentleman wearing a blue sports jacket and khaki slacks.

"I didn't hit him," the driver said. "It was close, but I *swear* I stopped in time."

"Jesse!" A frantic young woman in her early twenties came running from the park, peeling off a pair of yellow rubber gloves and tossing them on the ground. "Oh no! Oh my god, what happened?"

"It was my fault," the other boy cried. "I threw the ball too hard, and Jesse went to get it. But the car didn't hit him. He tripped and fell."

As sirens sounded in the distance, the small crowd stepped back far enough to let the distraught woman move in and kneel beside the injured child. Her eyes filled with tears as she took in the road-burn scrape on his forehead, the bruise on his cheek and the dribble of blood trickling down his nose.

Ramon placed an arm around on the woman's shoulder, clearly trying to comfort her. "I don't think it's as bad as it looks, Katie. I'm sure he's going to be okay."

Jesse attempted to sit up, but Ramon placed a gentle hand on his chest and stopped him. "Hold on, buddy. I don't think you should move until the paramedics can look you over. Okay?"

A young guy with purple-tinted hair and a variety of face piercings nudged Callie's arm. "What happened?"

"It looks worse than it probably is," Callie said. Then she explained how the boy had gotten hurt.

"Oh wow. *Scary.*"

Before Callie could agree, a deputy sheriff pulled up in his squad car, just as the Fire Department ambulance arrived, followed by a hook and ladder truck.

As two paramedics carrying their first-aid gear made their way past the onlookers, Ramon got to his feet and stepped aside to let them take over. He said something to Katie, and she nodded. Her once-panicked expression shifted into one that seemed grateful, and she mouthed, "Thank you."

Ramon placed his hand on her shoulder in a comforting way, then he moved to the back of the crowd, where the other boy stood, his face tear streaked, his body trembling.

The scene continued to unfold, with the para-medics taking vitals, Katie gazing worriedly at Jesse and the police officer talking to the harried driver. But Callie found herself more interested in watching Ramon, in observing the way he'd handled an emergency. He might not be medically trained, but he'd jumped right into the thick of the situation, taking charge like a city leader should.

Even now, as he placed his hand on the older boy's shoulder, offering comfort, he bore a heroic demeanor.

Callie continued to stand off to the side until Marianne, the woman wearing the lime-green shirt and still holding her pie and fork, approached her. "I hope that poor kid is going to be okay."

"I think he will be," Callie said. "I'm sorry about taking off like I did. I didn't mean to desert you."

"No problem. Helena and I went back into the café because we didn't want to get in the way. We're leaving now, but I left cash to cover the bill and a tip on our table."

"Thank you. I appreciate that." Callie really needed to go back inside, too—before her shift ended. But she couldn't seem to tear herself away from the drama that could have been so much worse.

"Callie," Ramon called out as he walked toward her, his hand on the uninjured boy's shoulder. "This is Mark. His little brother is going to be fine, but the paramedics want to take him to the ER as a precaution. I told their sister I'd keep an eye on him until she and his brother get home."

"That's nice," Callie said, although, even in an emergency, she would've been leery about leaving Mikey with a bystander. She figured most mothers would feel the same way—unless they knew their child would be safe. But a sister, she supposed, might not be that concerned. Unable to stifle her curiosity, she asked Ramon, "Are you a friend of the family?"

"Yeah, I guess you can say that."

Mark sniffled, then wiped his brow with his sleeve. "He's our baseball coach."

Ramon smiled at the kid and ruffled his scruffy dark hair. "And right now, I'm ready for that tri-tip sandwich I ordered. I'll bet Mark's hungry, too."

"Not really," the boy said. "Katie packed me

and Jesse a lunch to eat while she cleaned the bathrooms."

"Then how about some dessert?" Ramon asked the kid. "Pie, maybe? Or a bowl of ice cream? It wasn't that long ago that I was an active kid like you. It never hurts to take in some extra calories."

Mark brightened. "I love ice cream. Especially if they have chocolate."

"They did yesterday," Ramon said. "I needed some extra calories myself."

Callie would've been worried sick if it would have been Mikey in the street, paramedics hovering over him as they prepared to take him to the ER. And she would have wanted to go to the hospital with him, offering him love and comfort.

"Has someone contacted the boys' mother?" she asked Ramon.

"We don't have a mom," Mark said. "We live with our sister, and she takes care of us."

Callie had no idea what to say. She certainly couldn't ask the boy any of the questions that sprung to her mind—particularly what had happened to their mother. Had she died? Or had she abandoned her kids like Callie's mom had done?

"Katie's young," Ramon said, "but she's doing a great job with the boys."

"I'm sure she is." Callie's heart went out to the young woman who was going to follow the ambulance to the hospital. "And it looks like she left you in good hands, Mark. Let's go inside. I'll get that sandwich for your coach and a big bowl of ice cream for you."

Ramon ushered Mark toward the café door. He paused near the bench long enough to pick up a battered baseball that must have belonged to the brothers, the one Jesse had been running to catch.

Mikey had never had any interest in sports, and neither had Callie when she was a girl. Heck, she'd been lucky to find the time or the space to get her homework done.

Yet for some reason, as she entered the restaurant with the young ballplayer and his coach, she felt as if she'd somehow become part of the team.

While Callie returned to the kitchen, Ramon took Mark back to the table near the window, where he'd left his sweet tea. Melting ice had watered down the color, and beads of condensation had formed on the glass, creating a small puddle underneath. He reached for it anyway and took a hearty, thirst-quenching swig.

"Are you sure my brother's going to be okay?" Mark asked, inquisitive brown eyes searching Ramon's, seeking cut-the-crap honesty.

"I'm no doctor, but I'll bet that he'll be home for dinner. He took a hard fall in the street, so he'll be sore and a little scraped up. If that car had actually hit him, it would have been a lot worse."

"I think he tripped over his shoelaces," Mark said, folding his arms and resting them on the table. "They kept coming untied, and I told him to double knot them, but I don't think he did."

The two brothers were only a year apart and very close—much closer than most siblings. Ramon figured that was because the family of three had no choice but to band together after their mom died last spring.

"Maybe Jesse will take your advice from now on," Ramon said.

"I sure hope so." Mark lowered his head, and his shoulders slumped.

"Everyone knows how hard you try to look after your little brother, and it shows. You're doing a great job." Ramon reached out, covered one of Mark's small hands with his, gave it an easy squeeze, then let go. "Don't worry about him. He'll be playing catch with you before you know it."

Mark nodded, accepting Ramon's assurance, believing his words rang true.

"All right, guys. Here you go." At the upbeat sound of Callie's voice, Ramon looked up to see her carrying a plate with his tri-tip sandwich and fries in one hand, and a giant ice-cream sundae in the other.

Mark's jaw nearly dropped to the table, and his eyes brightened for the first time since his brother fell in the street. *"Oh man."* He looked at Callie. "Is that for *me*?"

She smiled and placed the bowl in front of him. "A little boy I once knew loved chocolate ice cream and whipped cream. And even though he was small for his age, he could really put it away. Something tells me you'll be able to finish this big helping, too."

"Don't worry. I can. I love ice cream. And fudge sauce." He turned to Ramon and grinned. "Hey, Coach. Look. It has whipped cream and *three* cherries on top."

Ramon chuckled, winked at Callie and said, "I see that."

The dark-haired boy, a great big grin stretched across his face, turned to Callie. "How did you know what I like?"

"Callie is the best waitress in the state," Ramon said. "It's like magic. She knows what her customers are going to order before they do."

Callie laughed. "I wouldn't call it *magic*."

"I would," Mark said. "Just about everyone on our team begs to go to the Pizza Palace after we win a game, but me and my brother ask to go to Doc Creamer's Frozen Delight instead. We like it better than going out for pizza. And you knew that."

"That's true." Ramon chuckled as he thought about the boys he coached. "It must be magic."

"Hey, Callie," Mark said, his spoon suspended

in midair. "That kid you used to know. The one who likes ice-cream sundaes. Did he play baseball, too?"

"No, he didn't. He wasn't into competitive sports."

"Why not?" Mark dipped his spoon into the bowl again, but his eyes remained on Callie.

She bit her bottom lip and seemed to ponder the question—or maybe her thoughts had drifted to the boy she used to know. Then, after a couple of beats, she seemed to shrug it off. "He wasn't very athletic. And sometimes the other boys would make fun of him, so he preferred indoor activities. Like reading."

Ramon couldn't stomach bullies, whether it was a child on the playground or a cocky loudmouth down at city hall.

"Sometimes kids, and even adults, can be mean to each other," Ramon told Mark. "And that's not cool. I hope that, if you ever see someone being pushed around or teased, you'll step up and tell 'em to knock it off."

"I already do that, especially if they pick on Jesse or his friends." Mark set down his spoon and caught Ramon's eye. "Were people ever mean to you, Coach? I mean, when you were a boy?"

"Sometimes guys would tease me. But not very often." Ramon picked up his tri-tip sandwich and took a bite. He'd always been one of the bigger kids. So most of the time, it only took a threat-ening glare to make a bully shut up and back off. Either way, whenever anyone got out of line, with him or with someone smaller or more vulnerable, he let them know he wasn't going to stand for it.

As Callie turned away from the table, Ramon called her back. "Don't go. You don't have any other customers right now. Sit with us for a while."

She glanced toward the kitchen, where Gloria, a retired Marine Corps sergeant, was probably doing prep work for the upcoming dinner hour. Gloria wasn't the owner of the café, nor was she Callie's boss, but sometimes she acted as if she were both.

"I don't want anyone to come in and find me sitting down on the job." She gave a little half shrug and smiled. "I can stand here and talk to you, though."

"Sounds good."

She glanced down at Mark, who was already digging into his bowl again—and doing a good job of convincing the adults that he planned to eat every last bite. Then she looked up and winked at Ramon.

Damn, she was pretty. And fun. He tossed her a boyish grin and asked, "What time do you get off work?"

The question had rolled off his tongue before he'd given any thought about what he might've implied. But he had to admit that he was tempted to spend some time with her—away from the café.

Callie glanced at the clock on the far wall. "I have about ten more minutes to go. That is, if Shannon, my replacement, gets here. She has a two o'clock class at the junior college today and sometimes she runs late."

"Then what will you do?" he asked. "Are you heading home to the family?"

"No. I'm off to the groomer's to pick up Rascal."

Not married? No kids? He reined in the compulsion to come right out and quiz her about her personal life, no matter how curious he might be. Instead, he asked, "So you have a fur baby? Or whatever it is animal lovers call their pets."

Callie's eyes lit up. "Rascal isn't a baby. He's about six years old, I think. And he's the sweetest dog ever."

Ramon could relate to another dog lover, even if he didn't have one of his own. When he was a kid, his father hadn't wanted one. And Jillian had been allergic to pet dander. Or so she'd said.

"What kind of dog is it?" he asked, as he reached for a french fry.

"The vet thinks he's a cross between a Queensland heeler and an Australian shepherd."

"No kidding?"

Her head tilted to the side. "You sound surprised. Why?"

He shrugged. "Because I thought you'd have something smaller, like a terrier or one of those fluffy-haired breeds that require a lot of grooming. Rascal is a cattle dog, and they usually live on a ranch."

Her eyes sparkled, and a grin stretched across her face. "Rascal *does* live on a ranch. We both do."

"Really?" Again, she'd blown another of his assumptions out of the water. "I thought you lived in town."

"No, I have to commute. My friend Alana Perez inherited the Lazy M Ranch a couple of months ago, along with Rascal, five cows and two horses. She didn't know anything about ranching, so she asked me to move out there and help her make a go of it."

"So you did?" He lifted a hand and snapped his fingers. "Just like that?"

She laughed. "Alana is my best friend, and she needed me. Besides, life had just thrown me a curve of my own, and I wanted to make a fresh start someplace else. So I left Texas, and here I am."

Ramon noted her baseball reference, but he was more interested in finding out what kind of curve she'd been thrown. She didn't elaborate, and in spite of his curiosity, he didn't ask. At least she seemed to be making the best of it—whatever *it* was.

He also admired her loyalty to her friend. "Since Alana asked for your help, I assume you grew up on a ranch. Or else you once lived on one."

At that, Callie laughed again. "No, I'm afraid not. I might be from Texas, but I'm a city girl. And so is Alana. She just knew she could count on me to help."

He slowly shook his head. He never would've guessed that, either. But then again, he'd only seen her wearing jeans and a Meadowlark Café shirt.

"You look stunned," she said. "And you're shaking your head as if you don't believe me."

"It's not that. It's just that…" He smiled and shrugged. "I'm trying to wrap my mind around what you're telling me. Two inexperienced city girls are trying to make a go of the Lazy M?"

"Alana and I might not have any experience, but you wouldn't believe how many things you can learn how to do from internet videos. And we've checked out a lot of books at the library. Besides, we're not quitters. And we're a lot tougher than you might think."

"I don't doubt that." But Montana winters could be brutal, and he wasn't sure how Callie and her friend would handle their first blizzard. He had to give them credit for trying, though.

"We've been learning something new every day," Callie said. "We may never turn the Lazy

M into the area's top cattle ranch, but we can make it somewhat productive."

Ramon struggled to reel in his surprise. "You two actually plan to run cattle?"

She shook her head. "Not right away. We know better than to jump into anything like that. We've planted a garden, though. And we bought some chickens. We're also doing some repairs around the place. Our biggest problem is that we're on a tight budget, so we're taking it one day at a time."

"That's admirable," he said. And considering the condition of the Lazy M the last time he'd been there, it was going to take a lot of work to get that ranch productive, not to mention a boatload of cash to refurbish that old house. Jack McGee, the previous owner, had suffered with arthritis for years and could barely take care of himself. But he'd been stubborn and had refused to sell or ask for help, and the ranch slowly went to hell.

Callie glanced at Mark, who'd just about finished his ice cream. A dab of whipped cream dotted his nose, and a smear of chocolate marred his cheek.

"Honey," she said, "you'd better go to the bathroom and wash your face and hands."

The boy pushed aside his bowl and reached for a napkin instead.

"It's going to take a lot more effort on your part than that," Ramon said. "If you don't use water, you're going to be a sticky mess. The bathroom is near the front entrance."

As Mark left the table, Callie turned to Ramon and smiled. "You're good with kids. You'll make a great father someday."

"I don't know about that." He shook off her praise and the pinch of resentment it provoked. He'd wanted kids, but Jillian hadn't. She'd claimed he wasn't mature enough to be a parent, that he wouldn't be "emotionally available" to a child. Whatever that was supposed to mean. Still, her claim had left his ego a little jaded about the whole daddy thing.

Callie furrowed her brow. "You're doubting that you'd make a good father?"

The question hit a little too close to home. "Don't get me wrong. I like kids, and I'm a good coach, but I don't know if I have the temperament to be a parent."

"I find that hard to believe. But then again, I suppose coaching a Little League team is a good way to find out."

"Maybe, but that's not why I coach the kids. I was an all-star pitcher in high school and then played college ball." He'd actually been good enough to get picked up by the majors, but he'd thrown out his shoulder when he'd been a junior, dashing that dream.

"Either way," Callie said, "the boys are lucky to have you."

Were they? He hoped so. But Jillian's accusations, the words she'd damn near shouted the night before she left, overrode Callie's kindhearted attempt to bolster his ego.

You're never there for me, Ramon. Your sports teams, your buddies and your dad always come first. And now that you've been appointed to fill that damned council seat, even the town has come between us.

Callie picked up Mark's empty bowl and turned to walk away, drawing Ramon's attention to the here and now, not to mention the soft sway of her shapely, denim-clad hips.

"Hey," he said, calling her back. "Where are you going?"

She stopped, glanced over her shoulder and grinned. "To get you a refill." She nodded to his nearly empty glass.

As much as he'd like to have her hang out at his table, she was still on the clock, and he didn't want her to get into trouble. Or lose her job. So he thanked her and let her go. Mark returned from the bathroom about the time Callie brought a pitcher of tea to the table and refilled Ramon's glass.

"Can I get you something else?" she asked. "Maybe a to-go box so you can take the rest of that sandwich with you?"

Ramon glanced down at his half-eaten meal. He'd been nearly starving when he'd first arrived at the café, but for some weird reason, he wasn't all that hungry anymore.

"That's a good idea," he said. "I can finish it later tonight."

When Callie returned to the table with the box, she also had his bill. "There's no rush on this. I'm leaving as soon as Shannon gets here, but feel free to stay as long as you like."

Ramon couldn't see any point in hanging out at the café once Callie left, so he reached into his pocket and pulled out a roll of cash, held together by his favored money clip—a rubber band that made it more difficult for a pickpocket to snatch. It was a trick he'd learned when he and Jillian lived in New York.

The front door squeaked open, and Shannon O'Malley walked in with a backpack slung over one shoulder and a purse hanging from the other. Her short black hair, the ends tinted pink, was disheveled, as if she'd had to run all the way from the junior college across town. Shannon not only worked part-time as a waitress at the Meadowlark Café, she was also the cook's niece.

"Hey, Cal," Shannon said. "I'm sorry I'm late."

Callie glanced at the clock on the far wall and gasped. "Uh-oh. You're right. I've got to get out of here. The groomer closes early today."

Shannon slipped behind the register and stashed her purse and backpack. "Is Gloria blowing steam out her ears yet? I was afraid to come in through the back door like usual. She really gets pissed when I'm late. So I thought I'd sneak in the front and pretend I've been here awhile."

Callie grinned and shook her head in amusement. Then she untied her apron and handed it to the young woman. "Here. Put this on. That way, you don't have to go into the kitchen until Gloria takes a cigarette break."

"Thanks, Cal. You rock."

Callie returned to the table and affectionately ruffled Mark's hair. "It was really nice meeting you. I hope you'll bring your brother in for an ice-cream sundae next time you're at the park. It'll be my treat."

Mark brightened. "I will. Jesse likes chocolate and whipped cream even more than me."

Ramon got to his feet. "Meet me at the cash register. I want to pay before you leave." He also needed change for a tip.

Once he'd paid with a couple of twenties, he handed a ten to Callie. "This is for you."

She turned a sky blue gaze on him. "This is too much."

"No, it's not. You've gone above and beyond today, and it's my way of thanking you." Yet he suspected she knew he felt more than appreciation and gratitude. "I'll see you tomorrow."

"Actually, I'm off until Sunday morning."

"Got a big date?" he asked, poking a stick at one of the many questions that had been niggling at him lately. But damn. He couldn't seem to help it. Hopefully, his attraction and interest wasn't obvious to her or to anyone else.

"The only date I have these days is with my doctor," she said.

Ramon's gut clenched, and his grin faded. She was seeing a doctor?

Regularly?

That didn't sound good.

"I'm just kidding," she added.

Was she? A comment she'd made earlier came to mind. *Life had just thrown me a curve of my own, and I wanted to make a fresh start.*

Like a change in doctors? A change in climate?

He hoped she wasn't sick. Or if she was, that whatever ailed her wasn't serious. It might not be any of his business, but the next time he had a chance to talk to her without an audience, he was going to come right out and ask her.

And that wasn't the only thing he had on his mind. He was also going to ask her out. Just not today...

Fairborn Ob-Gyn was located in a two-story, redbrick medical building across the street from

Town Square Park and adjacent to the ball fields. Callie originally had a nine o'clock appointment, but Dr. Patel had been called to the hospital to deliver a baby. As a result, his receptionist called her at 7:30 a.m. and said that he'd told her to reschedule his morning patients.

"How about next Thursday at two?" the woman asked.

"I hate to complain," Callie said, "but I've only been to your office once. Dr. Patel was out sick that day, so I saw the nurse practitioner. I haven't had an ultrasound yet. And I'm already fifteen weeks along."

"Then we'll squeeze you in this afternoon. Can you come in at four thirty?"

"Yes, of course."

Needless to say, Callie arrived early and eager. In fact, she was so excited to see an image of her baby that she'd wolfed down a quick lunch, which hadn't set very well and probably explained why she felt a little nauseous. For the most part, as long as she kept something light in her stomach, she felt okay. But if she ate too much or skipped a meal or a snack, her morning sickness struck with a vengeance.

She took a seat in the crowded waiting room, which had pale yellow walls and brown tweed furniture. An array of potted plants and a mural of a French countryside provided a cozy, peaceful feeling that seemed to ease her nerves and settle her stomach. But she still had to wait nearly forty-five minutes to be called back to an exam room and even longer yet for Dr. Patel to enter and introduce himself.

The balding, fiftysomething obstetrician had a warm smile and a friendly yet competent demeanor. "I'm sorry about the wait."

"No problem," Callie said.

When asked to lie back on the table, she complied and waited while the doctor felt her uterus. His brow furrowed, and she zeroed in on him.

"Fifteen weeks?" he asked.

"Yes. As far as I know."

He nodded. "Let's take a better look at your little one." He set up the machine, typed in her name and the date, then squeezed a glob of cold gel on her tummy.

Callie tried to make sense of the grainy black-and-white images, but she wasn't sure what she should be looking for.

Dr. Patel moved the sonogram wand over her belly, pressing it in, then stopping. "Well, I'll be. Would you look at that."

Oh no. Bile rose up in her throat, but nausea seemed to be the least of her problems.

"Is something wrong?" she asked.

"No, Mama. But brace yourself." The obstetrician looked up and smiled. "You're having twins."

Chapter Three

*T*wins?

A response wrapped itself into a knot of emotion in Callie's throat. All she could do was stare at the screen Dr. Patel was pointing at and study the two little babies in her womb, watching their hands and feet moving, their little hearts beating.

"Double the blessing," the doctor said in a voice that bore a hint of reverence.

Yes, she considered them blessings. Yet there'd also be double the expense and worries.

"Looks like you'll have one of each," he added, "a boy and a girl."

"I don't know what to say," she finally muttered. "I'm stunned."

The real questions would come later, she supposed, once she'd wrapped her head around the news that she'd be having two babies instead of one. Her thoughts vacillated between disbelief, joy and apprehension.

"How will the babies' father take the news?" the doctor asked.

Garrett hadn't wanted one child, let alone two. For the briefest of moments, Callie's anger at and frustration with the man, as well as the disappointment in herself for not seeing through his charming facade, struck hard. But she shook it off—all of it. She and her child—her *children*—were much better off without him in their lives.

"Their father isn't in the picture," she said.

"I understand. Several of my patients are single mothers, and a few of them are forming a support group. I'd be happy to give you a contact number for the woman who's organizing it."

Callie hadn't had much luck when it came to leaning on strangers when things were tough, so she wasn't about to do it now. Besides, she didn't need outside support. "I have a good friend who'll be there for me. And she'll be the best labor coach I could ever hope for."

"I'm glad to hear that." Dr. Patel wiped the cool gel from her belly, then offered her his hand to help her sit up. He touched her shoulder and gave it a gentle pat. "If you should change your mind about meeting some of the other new mothers, let me know."

She offered him a brave smile. "I will, Doctor. Thanks."

Once he left the room, Callie climbed down from the exam table, slipped off the hospital gown and got dressed. After she reached for her purse, she headed to the reception desk to make her next appointment. Then she left the office.

As she waited for the elevator to reach the second floor, she tried to come to grips with what she'd seen on the screen, what she'd face in the very near future.

Not that she was unhappy about the news. But she'd already been stressing about how to tell Mikey she was pregnant.

No, not Mikey. *Micah*, her brilliant med school–bound college student.

What would he say now? How would he feel when he learned he'd not only be getting a little brother, but a sister, too?

As Callie entered the elevator and pushed the first-floor button, she felt a buzz of excitement, as well as a tremor of nerves. She'd had a similar feeling two months ago when she'd looked at the calendar and realized she hadn't had a period in a while. She'd been so caught up with the upcoming move to Montana and renting out her small home in Texas that her menstrual cycle had completely skipped her mind.

That same conflicting emotion struck harder still when she'd taken a home pregnancy test and studied the apparatus until a dark blue plus sign formed.

She knew that having a baby would be a life-changing event, especially since she was already the mother of a teenager. But *twins*? She blew out a wobbly sigh.

A sense of panic threatened to overwhelm her. And yet, there was something about rocking a little one in her arms that provided a sense of warmth and peace. That's why, when Micah had gone off to college and she'd found herself an empty nester, she had begun to volunteer one evening a week at a home providing temporary emergency care for children who had to be separated from their families, either for their own safety or because their parents couldn't provide proper care. There she comforted the little ones who were awaiting family reconciliation or foster care.

As a child, Callie had spent a couple of months in a place like that—abandoned, afraid and apprehensive. She'd prayed her mother would come and rescue her even though, deep inside, she'd known her mom's addiction was too strong, that her desperate need for drugs wouldn't allow her to put her daughter's needs above her own.

At Casa de Niños, she used to rock fussy babies to sleep and hold toddlers on her lap, reading to them in a soft, gentle voice. It was her way of paying it forward. And if truth be told, the little ones weren't the only ones being comforted. Callie got a lot out of it, too. And she missed it.

She hoped to do the same thing at the Phelps Center in Kalispell and had an appointment this evening for an interview, although now she wasn't so sure she should be making a commitment like that. Her hands—or rather, her arms—were going to be full soon.

As the elevator rumbled to a stop, a wave of nausea swept through her again.

She reached into her purse, fumbling around for the saltine packets she'd been saving from lunch, only to come up empty-handed. Apparently, she'd eaten the last one in the waiting room.

Once she entered the lobby and was back on steady ground, she felt a little better. Going outside and breathing in some fresh air would help, too.

She took a moment to savor the soft mountain breeze whispering through the trees. The sound of children's voices drew her attention to the grassy area across the street and to the ball field, where a Little League team had gathered around their coach.

But it wasn't just any coach.

Callie stopped on the sidewalk and watched

Ramon for a moment, the way he stood, broad-shouldered, hands resting on narrow hips. He wore a red baseball cap, just like the boys on the field. He'd also dressed casually in a long-sleeved white T-shirt and a pair of faded jeans. Yet it was more than his physical appearance that appealed to her. She liked the way he interacted with the boys, the way they all seemed to look up to him.

Callie admired him, too. It took a special man to volunteer his time and help the youth in Fairborn.

If things were different, if there weren't so many obstacles to consider, like the age thing and Ramon's standing in the community, she might…

She placed a hand over her growing tummy, somewhat hidden by the fabric of her sundress.

No, she absolutely would *not* consider anything other than friendship with Ramon. The biggest obstacle holding her back was her pregnancy, which had been her secret so far. But it wouldn't be one much longer. She'd already begun to leave the top button on her waistband undone. And since she was carrying twins, she'd be expanding quickly. Still, she couldn't help watching the coach and the team from a distance.

Would either her new son or daughter be interested in sports? Would she cheer for them at baseball or soccer games?

The boys on Ramon's team began to disperse, picking up mitts and other belongings and heading to various parked cars. She knew she ought to do the same thing, to find her own vehicle and drive home, to not give all the what-ifs another thought.

But for some crazy reason, she turned and headed toward the ball field instead.

As the last of the parents drove off, Ramon turned to Jesse, who'd stuck by his side all during practice. A nasty knot on the boy's forehead and a scrape on his chin were stark reminders of his fall in the street yesterday, an accident that could have been so much worse than a few cuts and bruises and a mild concussion.

He'd begun to take the Johnson brothers under his wing soon after they'd joined the team and he'd learned they were orphans. But after having a chat with Katie at their house late last night and learning the elderly neighbor who'd been looking after the boys for her had moved across town, he'd decided to do whatever he could for the family.

An hour ago, when Katie had dropped the boys off at the ball field, she'd said, "I was only going to bring Mark today, but Jesse didn't want to miss practice. He's supposed to take it easy for a few days, but he hates going to study groups with me, especially microbiology. So, if you don't mind, I'd like to leave him here. He promised to sit on the sidelines and watch."

"No problem. I'll feed them after practice. Just

give me a call when you're on your way back to the apartment, and we'll meet you there."

Katie blew out a sigh of relief. "That would be awesome. Thank you so much." As she'd turned to go, she'd stopped and added, "I should only be there for two hours, but I could be a little late. My battery isn't too good, so sometimes my car won't start. I left it running in the parking lot here because I'll only be a minute, but I can't do that at the library. And I can't always find someone willing to give me a jump start."

Microbiology was a tough class. Ramon's college buddy had really struggled with it. Katie would need to stay on top of it if she wanted to become a vet. "I carry jumper cables. Just call me if the car gives you any trouble."

Her bright smile nearly put the sun to shame. "Thanks. You rock, Coach."

It was the least he could do to help. Katie had been attending the state university when their mom died, and even though she'd been barely twenty, she'd petitioned for, and won, custody of her younger half brothers. As a result, she'd had to drop out of school and give up an academic scholarship. She'd just begun to pick up a class or two each semester at the junior college across town. She was also working her butt off to keep a roof over their heads. Ramon hoped that through hard work and perseverance, Katie would eventually become the veterinarian she wanted to be.

Now, as the other boys dispersed and Mark and Jesse stood by his side, Ramon placed a hand on the boy's small shoulder. "How are you holding up?"

Jesse looked at him and smiled. "I'm okay, Coach. Why?"

"Your sister's pretty busy these days. She's got a couple of jobs, and those two college classes take up a lot of her time. So, after we go to Joe's Burger Junction, I'll stop by Tip Top Market and pick up a few staples for you guys to have on hand."

"Staples?" Jesse scrunched his face. "Why would we want *those*?"

Mark giggled. "We can't eat staples."

Ramon bit back a laugh. "I meant getting some of the basic foods, like bread, milk, eggs, butter. Maybe cereal and some canned goods."

"How about mac and cheese?" Mark asked. "That's my favorite thing to eat, even for breakfast."

"You got it, sport." Ramon tugged at the bill of the boy's cap. "Come on. You can help me gather up my gear so we can get out of here."

Mark nodded, then trotted off. Before Jesse could follow after his brother, Ramon placed a hand on his shoulder to hold him back. "You can help him, but I don't want you to run."

"Okay, Coach. I know the rules."

As Ramon picked up the last of the bases on the field, he glanced up to see Callie heading his way.

A lazy grin stretched across his face. She'd said she had a doctor's appointment today, and since the medical offices were located in Peterson Plaza, the two-story building across the street, she must have come right over. He was glad to see her here. And he was especially glad to see her long honey-brown hair hanging loose over her shoulders instead of confined in a bun. She had on a pale yellow dress for a change, rather than the jeans she wore to work. He'd figured that she'd look good outside the café. And damn. He'd been right.

As she approached, she tucked a glossy strand of hair behind her ear, revealing a pearl stud earring, and offered him a shy smile he found endearing.

"I was heading to my car in the parking lot and spotted you at practice," she said. "I thought I'd come by and say hello. I also wanted to ask about Jesse."

"He's supposed to take it easy for a few days, which he's not happy about, but he's doing okay." He nodded toward the boys. "We're going to grab a bite to eat—nothing fancy. Do you want to join us?"

She seemed to ponder the idea. Then she slowly shook her head—with a little regret, it seemed.

"I would," she said, "but I have an interview tonight at the Phelps Center."

"You're looking for a new job?"

"No. I'm going to volunteer my help, and they're expecting me in a few minutes."

"No kidding? That's cool." He was just about to ask what she would do there, but Mark ran up to him, Jesse only a few slow steps behind. Since the boys had spent a little time at the Phelps Center before Katie was granted custody, Ramon let it go for now. No sense bringing up tough memories.

"Coach," Mark said, "if you give me the keys, I'll put that stuff in your car."

Ramon shuffled the bases he held in his arms, reached into his front pocket for the remote and tossed it to the boy. Then he turned his attention and focus back on Callie. She might have had a doctor's appointment, but she certainly looked healthy. And pretty.

Had he made the wrong assumption when he'd assumed she might be sick? Was she actually *dating* a doctor?

Maybe. And that possibility presented a different dilemma. He'd sworn off women for a while, at least until after the upcoming election. He hadn't wanted the more conservative voters to come up with any imaginary or unsavory reasons for his divorce. But when he thought about Callie going out with someone else, that reason paled. Because when push came to shove, he didn't want to lose her before he had a chance to get to know her a lot better.

"Are you sure you can't find time for a quick bite?" he asked. "I'm taking the kids to Joe's Burger Junction. I'm really craving one of their double bacon cheeseburgers right now."

She turned a little green around the gills, threw her hand over her mouth, rushed toward a blue trash can and heaved her guts out.

Dammit. There *was* something wrong with her, and a slew of possibilities crossed his mind, each one more serious than the next. He dropped the bases to the ground, strode over to the trash can and gently placed his hand on her back. "You okay, Callie?"

She shook her head yes, although she continued to puke.

"Did you eat something that made you sick?" he asked. "Or did you pick up that flu bug that was going around town?"

She shook her head no. Finally, when she'd emptied her stomach, she straightened and said, "It's not…contagious."

Oh man. Not a virus, then. Was it serious? Was it…cancer?

God, he hoped not. But there were all types of doctors. In fact, he'd just started seeing a doctor himself lately. A counselor, actually. But only to bounce a few things off the guy so he could move on after his split with Jillian.

Maybe that's what Callie meant—maybe she was going through something that racked her guts emotionally. If that were the case, he'd respect her privacy. Hell, he drove nearly twenty-five miles away for his counseling sessions, just so no one in town would know what he was up to.

"Are you sure you're okay?" he asked.

Seriously? Callie wasn't the least bit okay, even if her stomach felt better now.

As Ramon's gaze locked on hers, demanding a response, the words balled up in her throat.

You'd think the answer would be obvious. She'd just lost her cookies in front of the guy she liked and the two little boys standing beside him, neither of whom seemed inclined to obey their coach and wait in the car. Instead, they'd watched while she leaned over a dirty, smelly trash can, trying to keep her hair out of the way of the mess and waiting for the dry heaves to stop.

Instead, she blew out a wobbly sigh. "Yes, I'm fine. Sorry about that."

"Don't be." Ramon slowly removed his comforting touch. "Can I get you something? A bottle of water? A wet paper towel?"

She appreciated his kindness and concern, but she had no idea how to respond to it. She'd always been the one to dole out compassion. She'd rarely been on the receiving end.

"Thanks," she said, "but I have a bottle of water in my car."

"If you're not feeling well, I can drive you home."

"Oh no." She took a wobbly step back. "You don't have to do that. It's just that I…I don't like bacon, and the thought of it made me sick." She managed a smile, but she kicked herself for coming up with such a lame explanation. Who threw up at the mention of a word?

Ramon turned to Mark and Jesse. "Hey, guys. The show's over. You can take the gear to my Expedition now. I'll be right behind you. And I'll bring the bases."

As the brothers made their way to the parking lot, dragging a green canvas bag behind them, Ramon's gaze snagged Callie's. "I've had breakfast at the Meadowlark Café at least once a week. I always order a side of bacon, and you've never made a mad dash to the restroom."

Okay. So he hadn't bought her explanation. She couldn't blame him. Anyone in their right mind would have been skeptical of a stupid excuse like that.

She really should level with him about her pregnancy and the occasional morning sickness that still plagued her at times. And she would do that soon. But she wasn't about to have that conversation with him while standing next to a trash can.

"I realize this isn't any of my business," he said. "It's just that you mentioned that you came from the doctor's office, and then you…" He nodded at the trash can. "You know. I hope whatever you have isn't serious."

"It's not. I promise. The appointment today was to establish me as a new patient. I just moved to town a couple of months ago, remember?"

He placed his hands on his hips, still skeptical, it seemed. Yet his compassionate gaze scrambled her heartbeats.

"I'm still worried about you," he said.

"Don't be." She forced a smile. "I'm already feeling much better. But on the outside chance I have a flu bug or something, I'd better call the Phelps Center and tell them I'm not coming in tonight." In fact, considering she was having twins and they could come early, maybe she ought to postpone her volunteer work.

Ramon continued to study her in a way that nearly caused her knees to give out, and she stole a glance at the trash can, just to make sure it was close enough to grab if she had to steady herself.

Darn it. She had to escape before she embarrassed herself any more—if that was even possible.

"If you'll excuse me…" She nodded toward the

restroom. "I'm going to wash my hands and face. I'll see you later. Have fun with the boys."

As she walked away, she hoped and prayed he'd be gone by the time she got out of the bathroom. But as luck would have it, even though she'd stayed inside the cinder block structure that housed the public restrooms for several extra minutes, she spotted him rooted in the very same spot, and her steps froze momentarily.

"You didn't have to wait," she said.

"I know, but I wanted to ask you a question."

She managed a faint smile. "What's that?"

"Are you free tomorrow night?"

Her lips parted, and her head tilted slightly off center. Was Ramon asking her *out*?

On a *date*? And after she'd just puked into a trash can?

It sure sounded that way, which was more flattering than he could probably guess. She had no idea what to say, but she couldn't just stand here, gawking at him.

"I don't have any big plans," she said. "Why?"

"Have you heard about the Silver Dollar Saloon?"

She caught a lot of local buzz working at the Meadowlark Café, but nothing about that particular place. The name was a dead giveaway, though. "Is it a bar?"

"It's a new restaurant that opened up about

twenty miles from here. It looks like a Wild West saloon, only a lot bigger, and has cowboy-themed dinner shows each night. From what I heard, it's a lot of fun."

She'd been prepared to turn him down, since she had no business dating anyone right now, but it had been ages since she'd gone out for the evening. And she had to admit she'd probably enjoy a show like that. And in all honesty, she'd like to see it with Ramon, even if that wouldn't be a smart move on her part.

"There's a piano man who plays ragtime tunes," he added. "And saloon girls dancing the can-can on stage. There's a comedian, a magician… I'm probably forgetting something. But I hear the food's good, especially if you like Texas-style barbecue. I'd like to check it out, but I'd rather not go alone."

Then…it *wasn't* a date. Ramon wanted a dinner companion, and so he'd asked her to go as a friend.

She bit her bottom lip and studied the handsome young councilman, trying to get a read on him. A boyish grin stretched across his face, dimpling his cheeks. Flecks of gold sparkled in his brown eyes, the color reminding her of rich, chewy caramel.

So sweet.

Yet sticky.

For some reason, going anywhere with him still seemed like a date, but she was hard-pressed to tell him no. Some woman was going to snatch him up in no time at all, and this might be her only chance to…

To *what*? Get dressed up and pretend she was going out on the town with a tall, dark and gorgeous hunk who had a way of making her laugh?

Get a grip, girl. Allowing romantic thoughts to cross her mind was downright wacky. The only ones getting any of her *sweet* kisses were the babies growing in her womb. And there was only one *sticky* position she would have to deal with, and that was when she had to tell her college-age son that he was finally going to be a big brother. And to a set of newborn twins.

Rather than make an assumption that could put one or both adults in an embarrassing or awkward situation, she said, "I'd love to go with you Ramon, but I really can't afford an expense like that right now."

His eye twitched, and for a moment, he appeared to be taken aback. Then his expression drifted to one of amusement, and he waved her off. "Dinner at the Silver Dollar Saloon is on me."

Talk about dancing around the elephant in the room. She wasn't any clearer about his intention than she was when he'd first asked her if she had plans tomorrow night.

"So, what do you say?" he asked.

Common sense urged her to say no, to come up with a good reason to backpedal. But after the stupid bacon excuse she'd just given him, she didn't trust herself to conjure up another one without giving it a lot of thought. Besides, she actually wanted to get out—and to get out with him, if she was being honest with herself.

She had enough to worry about these days. The last thing she needed was to consider dating, especially since a romantic relationship with Ramon wasn't going anywhere.

But it had been ages since she'd had any real fun. "All right," she said. "Should I meet you there?"

He waved her off yet again. "I'll pick you up at the ranch around six o'clock."

She merely nodded, even though she'd probably kick herself later. Then she headed toward her car, wondering what she ought to wear to a place like the Silver Dollar Saloon. Jeans, maybe. Or Western wear. But she damn well better not wear her heart on her sleeve.

Chapter Four

On the way to the ranch, Callie called the Phelps Center and told them she wasn't feeling well. Although fudging the truth made her a little uncomfortable, she was too overwhelmed by the news she'd just received, as well as her embarrassment over the public display of morning sickness, and she just wanted to go home.

Still, she decided to stop by Tip Top Market, where she purchased two boxes of saltines, one to have at the house and one to keep in the car. She ate a couple of crackers on the way home and, by the time she turned onto the long, graveled road that led to the ranch, she felt a whole lot better.

Callie had loved her small house in Texas—

which had belonged to her late aunt—but there just was something peaceful and welcoming about the Lazy M. Something that made her feel as if she'd just come home. Alana felt the same way, which was why she'd dubbed it Rancho Esperanza, Spanish for Hope Ranch, although most of the locals still referred to it as the Lazy M, either out of habit or respect for Jack McGee, Alana's late grandfather.

Life hadn't been easy for Alana, but her luck changed after she met her paternal grandfather. The two had connected through an ancestry DNA testing site and found out Alana was Jack's only living relative. Sadly, the seventy-three-year-old rancher had just been diagnosed with terminal lung cancer. Alana had taken care of him until the end—and then by leaving her the ranch, he'd given her a new beginning.

Alana had quit her job as a nanny, given up her apartment in Texas and moved in with Jack.

Callie had to give Alana credit, especially since she knew nothing about ranching or cattle. But Alana firmly believed the ranch offered her a chance to create a better future for herself—and for anyone who might want to join her there. Alana had the passion and determination to turn things around, but she lacked the resources. Hopefully, things would come together for her before she ran out of funds.

After parking near the weathered red barn that needed work, not to mention a fresh coat of paint, Callie climbed from the car. She glanced to her right at the six scraggly cherry trees on the east side of the yard—an orchard, if you could call it that. Even after years of neglect, they'd begun to sprout blossoms. A sign of new life and hope, she supposed.

As she made her way to the house, Rascal hurried out of the barn to greet her, his tail wagging, the red bow the groomer had tied around his neck yesterday drooping.

"Hey, sweet boy." She bent to give the cattle dog a scratch behind the ears. "Let's go inside. I'll bet Alana has dinner ready for both of us." The dog trotted along beside her as they entered through the back door, into the mudroom and into the kitchen, where Alana stood in front of the stove, peering into a pot.

"Something smells good," Callie said.

Alana turned away from the stove, a smile dimpling her cheeks, her green eyes bright. "I found my grandmother's old recipe book this afternoon. It's pretty cool. She made little handwritten notes inside. I mean, it's not like I found her diary, but it's another way for me to get to know her and to get some kind of an idea what growing up on the Lazy M might have been like."

Living with Jack and Mary McGee definitely

would have provided Alana with a happier and better childhood than the one she'd had. The only downside was that she would have grown up in Montana, which meant it wasn't likely that she and Callie would have met. And their friendship had given them both strength and the ability to deal with almost anything life threw at them.

"So what's in the pot?" Callie asked.

"Chicken and dumplings. Apparently, that was Grandpa's favorite meal."

"I can't wait to try it." Callie hung her purse on the back of one of the kitchen chairs and put the box of saltines in the pantry.

"I've seen pictures of my grandmother," Alana said, "and I have some of her things, like her sewing kit and her Bible. And now I have her recipe book. They all give me a little insight into the kind of person she was."

"At least you got to know your grandfather."

"That's true," Alana said. "He and my mom had been really close, especially after my grandmother died. So he kept thinking she would eventually come home, that they'd patch things up. But she never did. That's why he joined the DNA registry. He'd almost given up hope until I contacted him."

"It would have been sad if your grandfather had died alone, not knowing about you."

"It also helped him to know that my mother

might have contacted him years ago, but she died right after I was born."

"Did he ever tell you why she ran away from home?"

"Grandpa Jack didn't approve of my dad. My mom was only sixteen, and my dad was in his twenties. He'd also been in trouble with the law back then, which was no surprise, especially since he ended up doing time in prison a few years later. Grandpa and I did the math, and it appears that she was about four or five months pregnant when she left." Alana tucked a strand of long, wavy dark hair behind her ear. "Speaking of babies, how did your first doctor's appointment go?"

"I like Dr. Patel," Callie said. "He seems nice and answered all of my questions."

"Good. I'm glad you're happy with him."

Callie took a seat at the table and blew out a sigh. "Yeah, but the ultrasound turned up a surprise."

"Uh-oh." Alana crossed the room, her brow furrowed. "You're not smiling. You're concerned about something. What's wrong?"

Callie paused, still trying to wrap her mind around the news. "It wasn't bad news. Just unexpected. And a little…unsettling." She swallowed. "I'm going to have twins."

"Wow." Alana froze in her tracks. Once she picked her jaw up from the floor, a slow smile began to stretch across her pretty face. "That must have been more than a surprise."

Callie sighed. "The pregnancy was unplanned, but this put it on steroids."

"What are you afraid of?" Alana asked as she pulled out the chair closest to Callie and took a seat. "You've been pregnant before, so you know what to expect."

"Not with twins."

"You'll be fine. And you've been a single mother—a darn good one."

"I know. But…it's not that."

"Are you thinking about that deadbeat baby daddy?"

"No. He's long gone and forgotten." Callie closed her eyes. "It's…Micah. When he went off to college, it's like I lost him. Don't get me wrong. I'm glad to know he's growing up and pursuing his dreams. But what if he…" Fear wrapped around the thought, and her words trailed off.

"He'll definitely be surprised," Alana said, "but give him a little time. He'll come around."

"Will he? What if he's embarrassed? Or angry and resentful? What if he…"

"Doesn't like you anymore? Doesn't respect you?" Alana reached out, took her hand and gave it a gentle squeeze. "That boy loves you, and even if he struggles with the news, he's not going to reject you. He'll always love you. And he'll learn to love those babies, too."

"You're probably right. But…what if he doesn't understand? My relationship with the baby daddy, the unplanned pregnancy… What if he thinks I'm an idiot? I can't lose him, I just can't." Again, Callie bit back tears, but Alana knew her too well.

"Look. You being a foster kid was hard. And you're always trying to prove yourself worthy, lovable. A fear of rejection tends to be your default mode. I get it. It's mine, too, Cal."

The truth hit her like a ton of dirty diapers. "Living with a family that isn't your own sucks." Callie managed a smile. "And then there was Aunt Rhonda, the ice queen."

"Your aunt loved you, even if you didn't feel it. I know she wasn't the most affectionate person in the world, but she had her own demons to deal with. Just keep in mind that, even though she didn't have to, she took you in and provided you with a home. She also let me stay with you guys. You and Micah were her only family, and she showed that by leaving her house and savings to you."

"True." What would Callie do without Alana's sense of reason and common sense? "You should have stayed in school. You'd make a great shrink."

Alana laughed. "No, that would have been a

bad idea. I would have spent too much time psychoanalyzing myself."

"Don't forget about me," Callie said, her mood lightening. "Between the two of us, you wouldn't have had time to see any other patients."

"I know. Right?" Alana winked. "Don't worry about Micah. He'll get used to the idea. And I'm sure he'll be cool with it."

"I hope you're right."

"I am." Alana got up from the table, but before returning to the stove, she stopped. "There's an upside. Remember how Micah used to beg you for a brother or sister?"

"Yes, but he was a kid back then. And he wanted someone his own age to keep him company."

"I know. Silver lining alert. The twins will already have built-in playmates."

"True. Thanks for putting things in perspective. I have a lot to be thankful for. I just have to get past the difficult stuff, like the extra cost of buying two of everything. And finding good day care."

"I'm here for you, Cal. Together, we'll make this work. And those babies will have more love than they know what to do with."

"Thanks. You rock."

"Hey. That's what friends are for. And don't forget, I'll do anything for you. Just ask. Promise?"

How could she not? It went against her core to

ask for help, but not when it came to the best friend she'd ever had. "I promise."

Alana tossed her a misty-eyed grin. "I'll have dinner on the table in no time. I know you need to get over to the Phelps Center."

"You don't have to hurry on my account. I called and told them I couldn't come in tonight." Callie made her way to Alana's side. "What can I do to help?"

"There's some of the herbal tea you like chilling in the fridge. You'll find a green salad and dressing in there, too. Would you please take them out?"

"Of course."

While Alana set the table, Callie removed the requested items from the fridge, tossed the salad at the kitchen counter and then placed it all on the table.

"So how'd your day go?" Callie asked.

"Busy, but it was productive. I registered to attend a beef cattle symposium they're having in Colorado next weekend. Hopefully, I'll learn something and it'll be worth the added expense."

"I'm sure it will be a good investment."

"By the way," Alana said, "I got a call from a guy who offered to buy the ranch. He's a big rancher in Texas who wants to expand his holdings by purchasing property in other states."

It would make sense for Alana to sell, even

though she was fully invested in her dream and determined to make a go of the old Lazy M.

"What'd you tell him?" Callie asked.

"That Rancho Esperanza isn't on the market. This is my only tie to family, and I don't care if he offered me a million dollars more than it was worth, I wouldn't sell."

It might take that much money to get the place up and running again. Jack McGee had been crippled by arthritis prior to his cancer diagnosis and hadn't been able to put in much physical labor, so Alana and Callie had their work cut out for them.

"I have a question for you," Callie said. "Have you ever heard of the Silver Dollar Saloon?"

"I think it's a cowboy-themed restaurant with a dinner show of some kind. Why?"

"Ramon asked me to go with him on Friday night."

"Oh yeah?" Alana reached for the salad bowl and took a second helping. "That should be fun."

"I think so, too." Callie took a sip of tea.

"You really like him, don't you?"

Callie had never said as much, but it was true. She did like Ramon. Too much. And if she were talking to anyone other than her best friend, she'd deny it. "He's got a great personality and makes me laugh. There's a lot to admire."

"It sounds as if he likes you, too."

"I get that feeling. But he's too young for me.

Besides, he could have his choice of women. What would a single guy in his twenties want with a pregnant single mother whose firstborn is already in college?"

"Oh, come on, Callie. Micah's only sixteen. And you were just a kid when you had him. How much older than Ramon do you think you are?"

"I don't know. Six years, maybe. Seven?" Callie reached for her fork and took a bite of the chicken. "Hmm. This is really good. My hat's off to your grandmother and her recipe book."

"Thank you. But let's get back to that good-looking councilman who makes you laugh. He's not that young. And he's also one of the city leaders."

"Yes, I know. And he seems to be a really good guy. He coaches youth sports teams and even plays in a men's baseball league on Saturday mornings. He clearly enjoys manly, outdoor activities. But that's another concern. What kind of father figure would he make for Mikey?"

"He prefers to be called Micah," Alana reminded her.

Callie shook her head. "Yes, I know. Old habits are hard to break. Anyway, Micah was a sweet brainy kid who preferred to read in his free time. And he's never been very playful. Gosh, Alana, even you said he seemed like a grown-up when he went off to kindergarten."

"And that pint-size grown-up is going to be a world-class brain surgeon before you know it. He doesn't need a stepfather. In fact, he probably never did."

No, he'd needed a father, but his had died before he was born. Derek Hedstrom. Callie had been heartbroken when she'd heard about the accident, although she hadn't been surprised. The handsome brainiac who'd tutored her in AP Calculus had had a wild side, one she'd found a little too exciting back then.

Who knew what Derek might have accomplished if he'd focused on getting into an Ivy League college rather than throwing back beers and racing motorcycles?

"Either way," Alana said, "I think Ramon will be a good friend. And someone to have in your corner."

Callie agreed. She imagined he'd make someone a good husband. But then again, his wife had left him for some reason, and she couldn't help wondering why.

Maybe Ramon had flaws the people in town hadn't seen. After all, who really knew what went on behind closed doors? Not that it was any of Callie's business, but no one had seen that divorce coming. She'd overheard various townspeople trying to connect the marital dots, but Ramon was the only one who had the answers.

And apparently, he wasn't talking.

* * *

Ramon had known that the Silver Dollar Saloon wasn't the kind of place most men would take a woman on a first date, which was why he'd thrown out the idea. If things didn't turn out the way he thought they might, he could still play it off as a non-date.

But there was little chance of that happening, he realized, as he sat across from a bright-eyed, smiling Callie at a round wooden table near the raised stage. The owners of the fun-filled establishment had spared no expense to recreate a modernized version of a Wild West theater, with hardwood floors and white walls adorned with nineteenth-century artwork.

A cowboy bar stretched the length of one wall, and an ornate stage with brass fixtures, antique lights and a plush red velvet curtain sat front and center, not more than twenty feet from their seats.

Enthusiasm buzzed as the audience filed into the spacious room and found their tables. But Ramon was more interested in the beautiful woman who'd come with him. He watched her happy expressions as she took in the colorful setting. When she caught him looking at her, she tossed him a dazzling smile.

"This is awesome," she said. "Thanks so much for inviting me."

He threw a grin right back at her. "I'm glad you came."

Moments later, the house lights dimmed, and the stage lit up. A woman wearing a long white gown and a perfectly coiffed dark wig introduced herself as Annie LaGrange, the owner of the saloon, and welcomed them to the Silver Dollar. Then she called a magician onstage. The audience gasped in delight at his amazing acts, some of which included a rabbit and several white doves. Next up was a ragtime piano player who played a number of knee-slapping tunes that had them all tapping their feet, singing along and swaying in their seats.

Five saloon girls wearing low-cut dresses, fishnet stockings and black ankle boots came out. They danced the can-can and punctuated their routine by doing the splits.

The first half of the show ended when two masked cowboys, their pistols raised, tried to rob the bartender and threatened to take a saloon girl hostage. A shoot-out erupted, and the sheriff saved the day.

During intermission, the waitstaff served the meals they'd ordered earlier from a menu offering a choice of barbecued beef, chicken or pork, as well as chuck wagon beans and slaw. By the time they'd eaten their fill, Ramon didn't think either of them would have room for dessert, but Callie surprised him when she suggested they split the apple pie à la mode.

As she dug into the vanilla ice cream, she lifted her spoon, pointed it at him and said, "You're going to have to roll me out of here." Her blue eyes glimmered, and a smile dimpled her rosy cheeks, making her look as pretty and happy as he'd ever seen her.

"I don't care if I have to rent a forklift to get you out of here. It's good to see someone serving you for a change. Eat up and enjoy."

Callie gave him a playful sock on the arm, showing him a fun-loving side he hadn't seen very often. Damn, he was glad she'd accepted his invitation.

When the second half of the show began, Annie LaGrange, who'd changed into a red velvet gown, sang a solo that nearly brought down the house.

A comedian, who called himself Bobby the Kid and claimed to be Billy's white-sheep relative, was a hoot.

The show lasted three hours, one of which was taken up by the dinner served during sets. Yet the night seemed to wrap up too soon.

"That was the best evening I've had in a long time," Callie told Ramon. "I've never laughed so much."

"Thanks for coming with me. It was a lot more fun having you here with me." And he wasn't just blowing smoke. He couldn't remember when he'd had such an enjoyable evening. But then again, he'd never taken Callie out.

As they left the building and headed to the parking lot, Ramon couldn't deny his attraction or the spark he felt whenever their eyes met. He might have told her this evening wasn't a date, but that's exactly what it had turned out to be. And, hopefully, she agreed. Because it felt like a good-night kiss was definitely in order—at least, if she agreed about that, too.

Chapter Five

After Ramon turned onto the county road and neared the Fairborn city limits, he stole a glance across the console at Callie, who seemed unaware of just how pretty she was, how appealing. Each time he saw her, spent time with her, he found himself more intrigued by her.

As if she'd heard his thoughts, she turned to him and smiled. "I can't remember when I had so much fun. I'll bet Mark and Jesse would have enjoyed the show."

"They sure would have. They don't get a chance to do things like that very often." In fact, if he hadn't paid their Little League registration fees, they wouldn't have been able to join the team.

"Katie tries hard to provide them with a normal life, but she can't always afford the extras."

"I admire you for taking them under your wing," Callie said. "You really have a way with kids."

Did he? "I'm not so sure I have any special gift or skill. Working with kids is easy when the boys and I have a love of baseball in common."

"Don't downplay what you're doing for all the boys on your team, especially Mark and Jesse."

He shot another glance across the console and caught her eye. Her warm smile bolstered his ego, which hadn't quite recovered from his split with Jillian.

"I'm not doing that much," he said.

Callie turned in her seat, facing him. "But you *are*, especially for kids who don't have a father in the house. Just spending time with them, listening, praising and encouraging them is huge."

"I don't mean to discount what I'm doing. It's just that I'm benefiting from the time I spend with them, too."

"I'm sure you are," she said. "I get a warm, peaceful feeling when I volunteer with foster kids, even though I usually get a little sad when I have to leave."

"For me, that's part of it. But…" He stopped in midsentence. Up until now, he'd kept his mouth shut about the reason for his divorce, except for what he'd told his dad. And while he still wasn't about to spill his guts to Callie, he trusted her enough to share more than he had with anyone else. Besides, if they should end up dating, she deserved to know what had gone wrong.

"I don't like talking about my personal life," he said, "but I'm a born competitor, and coaching the team makes me feel a little bit better about the fact that I couldn't hold my marriage together."

"You blame yourself?" she asked.

"Not entirely. It's complicated, I suppose." His fingers squeezed the steering wheel, then he eased his grip. "We met in college. Jillian was a theater major. I'd gotten a baseball scholarship and had hoped to play pro ball after graduation, but a torn rotator cuff screwed up that plan. I went on to get an MBA and got a good job on Wall Street as an investment banker." He shot a look at Callie, only to see her gaze locked on him, listening intently as he continued, "I was working crazy hours, but making money hand over fist. And Jillian kept landing parts in off-Broadway plays. We rarely saw each other, but it didn't seem to matter, especially since she enjoyed the theater life."

"So why'd you move back to Fairborn?"

"My parents split up when I was young. My mom left and my dad raised me on his own. He and I have always been close. So when I found out he'd scheduled a hip replacement, I told Jillian I was going to take a leave of absence in order to help out on the ranch while he recovered."

"How'd she take it?"

"She understood. She had a big part in a musical at the time and told me to go without her. Then, a few days later, she fell during a dance routine and tore a couple of ligaments in her knee. Since she was going to need some downtime to heal, she agreed to go with me. That's when things changed."

"How so?" Callie asked.

"Not long after we arrived, I learned about the political corruption and the town's financial problems. So I told Jillian I wanted to put in my two-week notice at the firm and stay in Fairborn."

"I'd think that she would appreciate your loyalty to your hometown."

Callie probably would have felt that way, but not Jillian.

"I hope you don't think I'm bragging," he said, "but when I was in high school and the captain of the baseball team, we went to state finals. People around here looked up to me. So I knew, with my influence, I could turn things around and put Fairborn back on the map."

"That's not bragging," she said. "I hear things at the Meadowlark Café. And there are plenty of people who agree with you, including me. You've made some big changes at city hall—good ones."

"Thanks for the vote of confidence." Ramon turned onto the road that led to the Lazy M and parked near the house. "After Jillian's knee healed, I suggested that she get involved with the community theater, but you'd think I'd suggested trading the diamond in her ring for cubic zirconia. Before long, she grew to hate small-town life and complained about the time I spent away from home. She claimed that my ambition and the town always came first."

"Was that true?" Callie asked.

"In some ways. But it wasn't just that. When we lived in New York, my focus on the firm and my career didn't bother her a bit."

"Did you consider counseling?"

"We both went for a while, but we stopped when we realized it wasn't going to work." Ramon shrugged. "She was the first to suggest divorce, and I knew that's where the marriage was headed, but I told her we should wait and try to work things out."

Ramon slowly shook his head as he recalled her reaction to that suggestion. *Seriously? Don't give me that crap. You're not that interested in working things out. You're more concerned about the effect a divorce will have on your standing as a small-town hero.* She'd been right, and the truth had stung.

"It takes two to end a marriage," Callie said.

"And for what it's worth, everyone thinks you've done an amazing job, and I wouldn't be surprised if you were elected mayor."

"I hope you're right." Ramon turned in his seat. Had they been seated on a sofa, without the console between them, their knees might have touched.

The light from the outside of the barn cast a glow in the vehicle, making her appear almost angelic as she sat in the passenger seat, kindness and compassion sketched on her pretty face.

"Just so you know," he said, "I'm not like some politicians. I put my heart into every campaign promise I make."

"I don't doubt that for a minute." She blessed him with a smile that made him glad he'd opened up, that he'd shared his guilt over the divorce and his intent to move on with his life.

"Anyway," he said, "that's pretty much the reason things went down they way they did. And after one last, late-night argument, she packed her bags, told me her lawyer would be in touch and then drove off."

"At least the two of you split before having kids," Callie said.

"True. That would have made it a lot worse."

"Do you ever think about having children in the future?" she asked, her voice soft, almost wistful.

"I really haven't given it much thought." Mostly because he wasn't entirely sure he could pull off being a good husband. That was, if he ever got married again. "I probably make a better coach than a father. The boys on my team look up to me, and I'm okay with that."

Callie nodded, as if she understood all he'd shared, then she reached for the door handle. They both climbed out of his SUV, and he walked her to the door.

He hadn't planned to jump into another relationship until the dust settled on his divorce, but that was before he'd spent the evening with Callie.

When they reached the front door, she turned to him and tucked a strand of hair behind her ear. "I had a good time. One of the best ever."

"Thanks for going with me." He eased closer to her, wondering what she'd say when he tried to kiss her. Or would that scare her away?

Maybe he ought to ask how she felt about it, but the closer he got to her, the more her soft, floral scent snaked around him, the stronger the urge to kiss her grew. Unable to help himself, he cupped her cheek, then brushed his mouth across her lips, letting her know how much he'd enjoyed being with her tonight, how much he'd like to go out with her again.

As she slipped her arms around him and kissed him back, he lost himself in her scent. The kiss deepened, and her lips parted, allowing his tongue to slip into her mouth. Damn. She tasted good.

She *felt* good. Something about her, about this, felt right.

As determined as he'd been to avoid dating, a celibate lifestyle was no longer feasible. He was definitely going to have to rethink his prior game plan.

And he didn't care what his constituents might think.

That was, until Callie stiffened, placed her hands on his chest, pushed him back and tore her mouth from his.

"I'm sorry. We can't…" She shook her head and glanced down at her feet, those pretty locks nearly hiding her face. "I can't."

"Did I overstep?"

She looked up, her eyes locking in on his. "No. I *under*stepped. I should have told you something sooner than this."

His brow furrowed. "What's that?"

She hesitated, clearly searching for the right words. "Ramon…I'm pregnant."

Callie expected Ramon to bolt, but he seemed stunned to the bone. And she couldn't blame him.

With an expression that was a little tough for her to read, he raked his hand through his hair, mussing it in an appealing way. "Wow. I…I don't know what to say."

"Neither do I." She had the urge to reach up and

smooth his hair, but she fingered the shoulder strap of her purse instead.

His head tilted slightly. "The father...?"

"He lives in Texas, where he intends to stay. He's not a part of my life. Not anymore."

He glanced at her waist, which had thickened. But probably not enough for anyone else but her to notice. "How far along are you?"

"About four months. I didn't find out until after I moved to Montana." She hated to make him squirm or to see him make a mad dash to his car, but she might as well make the rest of the announcement. "The other day, when you were coaching the kids at the park, I'd been to the doctor's office, where I found out that I'm having twins."

He blew out a slow whistle.

She waited for him to speak. When he didn't, she said, "You're a great guy. And I like you. A lot. But now you can see why I was dragging my feet about dating."

He slowly nodded, agreeing with her, it seemed. "Does the father know anything about this?"

"Yes, but only that I'm pregnant. Like I said, he's long gone. We broke up before I even knew about the baby. And when I called to tell him, he told me to 'get rid of it.'"

Ramon scrunched his brow, and his eye twitched.

Callie leaned against the front door and blew out

a sigh. "I only told him because I thought he had the right to know. And while I didn't expect him to be happy, I had no idea he would be so cold and callous. If we'd been talking to him in person, I might have told him off. And maybe even punched him. But as it was, we were nearly two thousand miles apart—and I'd like to keep it that way."

"So there won't be any custody issues?"

"None whatsoever. He's a businessman I met over the holidays. He was staying in Dallas while he opened a satellite office. The day we met, I was feeling a little lonely, so when he asked, I agreed to go out with him. We went to dinner and…I guess I was flattered by his attention."

"You deserve to be wined and dined," Ramon said. "And often. But not by a guy who won't assume responsibility for a child he helped create. Or, in this case, two of them."

"Thanks. But just to be clear, I hadn't done much dating since I was in high school. And I hate to admit this, but for some crazy reason, I believed everything he told me about himself. I actually thought I'd finally found Mr. Right. But then I noticed a few holes in his story. I followed my instincts and did some research."

"What did you find out?"

"That he was married and had three kids. So I ended things immediately. When Alana asked me to come to Montana, I jumped at the chance to put some distance between me and the biggest mistake I'd ever made. Then, a few weeks later, I realized I was pregnant."

"Does he know you're not only keeping the baby, but that there are going to be two of them?"

"No. It wouldn't matter to him either way. His wife's family has money, so he'd hate for anyone to know he'd been messing around, which would probably lead to a divorce. So, like I said, he's history. And for what it's worth, I was more angry than brokenhearted when we split." Oddly enough, she felt much better now that she'd leveled with him. And maybe even better about the news itself. She straightened, her back still to the door, but standing tall as she continued to face Ramon. "I'm looking forward to having the babies."

"Then I'm happy for you." His smile appeared genuine, which was a relief.

Hopefully, her pregnancy wouldn't affect their friendship, although it might get a little awkward when he began to date other women. But being Ramon's friend would be enough. It would have to be.

"If there's anything I can do to help," he said, "let me know."

His kindness was sweet, and she'd have to count herself lucky that he wanted them to remain friends. Yet a pang of regret gripped her chest.

"I'd better let you go," Callie said, the truth of those words resounding in her heart long after she told Ramon good night and went into the dark, empty house alone.

After dropping the bombshell on Ramon Friday night, Callie hadn't expected to see him at the Meadowlark Café anytime soon, if at all. He'd offered to help her in any way he could, but she suspected he'd only wanted to soften the blow of his complete disappearance from her life.

She couldn't blame him for wanting to steer clear of her. After that blood-stirring kiss they'd shared, any bachelor in his right mind wouldn't want a pregnant woman to get the wrong idea about his intentions, especially when the mommy-to-be was carrying twins.

But on Sunday morning, while Callie stood at the corner booth and took a breakfast order from Helena Davis and Marianne Posey, the front door squeaked open. Out of habit, Callie glanced up from her notepad to see who'd just arrived and bit back a gasp.

Ramon strolled into the café dressed casually in black boots, worn jeans and a Western-style blue plaid shirt. On the weekends he looked more like a handsome cowboy than a town councilman. And today was no different.

When he spotted her, he lobbed a boyish grin at her in a way that sent her heart tumbling across her chest like a gymnast on a floor mat. As he made his way toward his favorite table, the one she'd always been assigned to service, her cheeks warmed.

Apparently, he wasn't avoiding her. That seemed a bit odd, but it pleased her.

Somehow, she managed to recover from her surprise and read back the orders she'd jotted down for the fortysomething women.

"Uh-oh." Marianne, whose red hair could use a touch-up, placed her elbows on the table, leaned forward and lowered her voice. "Don't look now, Helena. But Ramon's here. And Eddie just walked in behind him. Would you feel better if we canceled our order and went down the street to the doughnut shop instead?"

"Oh crap." Helena paled, then lifted the menu to shield her face. "Maybe I'd better make a mad dash out the back door."

"That was months ago," Marianne said. "He's probably forgotten all about it."

"Not a chance." Helena rolled her eyes. "After the scene I made at the Blue Moon Inn?"

Marianne clicked her tongue, then looked up at Callie, lowered her voice and said, "Helena spotted him with a sexy young blonde and accused him of being a womanizer. Then she threw a drink in the woman's face."

Curiosity slammed into Callie, and after the big mistake she'd made, after trusting her attraction to a man who'd pretended to be a nice guy and ended up being a jerk, she lowered her own voice and asked, "Was Ramon still married when you saw him out with the blonde?"

"Ramon?" Helena scrunched her face. "He wasn't even there that night."

At that, Marianne let out a little chuckle. "Helena used to date Eddie Cruz, Ramon's father. And things didn't end well between them. Since she was nursing a broken heart, a couple of us made her go with us to the Blue Moon Inn, and she had a few too many drinks."

"A *few*?" Helena rolled her eyes. "I was bombed out of my mind. I'm not a drinker, so they suggested I order a Long Island Iced Tea. Those might sound mild and taste good, but I had no idea how potent they were."

Marianne reached across the table and placed her hand over the top of Helena's. "You're allowed to have fun with your friends. And we had a designated driver."

"I know, but that's not an excuse to get that damned drunk and to flip out like I did."

Marianne glanced at Callie and shrugged. "We'd been there awhile, and then Helena saw Eddie out with another woman. It hadn't been very long after their breakup, and she assumed he'd left her for someone else. So she marched over to their table and… Well, let's just say she raised quite a ruckus.

So she's been trying to avoid Eddie and anyone who knows him."

"I've also been avoiding the Blue Moon Inn," Helena added, her menu still lifted to hide her face. "They eighty-sixed me that night. And now that I've paid for the damages, I'm allowed to go back. But the whole thing was terribly embarrassing, especially since the bar had caught it all on video, and they played it in court."

As wild as that evening must have been, Callie couldn't help feeling a wee bit sorry for the poor woman and offered her a warm smile. "So what do you ladies want to do about breakfast? Should I place your order?"

"No," Helena said, "you'd better not. This is the second time I've crossed paths with Ramon here, and to make matters worse, there's Eddie himself. Damn. Now I'm going to have to avoid the Meadowlark Café, too. At least until things blow over. And that might take a long time."

"Oh, for crying out loud," Marianne blurted out. "You can't avoid Eddie forever. Besides, you apologized to him when you saw him in court. And you haven't given him any trouble since."

Helena blew out a weary sigh, then lowered the menu. "You're right. I need to get over the embarrassment. Okay, Callie. We'll eat here—quickly. And I just won't make eye contact with him."

Callie ripped the top sheet from her notepad.

"Then I'll take your order to the kitchen and ask Gloria to get right on it." Once she did, she'd pick up the carafe from the coffee maker so she could serve Ramon and his father. She'd like to get a better look at the man who'd broken Helena's heart.

Was he the womanizer Helena had accused him of being when she'd seen him at the Blue Moon Inn? Or had a broken heart and several drinks caused her to have an out-of-character outburst?

Moments later Callie got her chance when she approached Ramon's table with the coffee, her gaze moving from the handsome young councilman to his equally attractive father. Both men had square jaws, expressive brown eyes and dark hair, although Eddie's had a splash of gray at the temple. The strong resemblance between father and son provided Callie with an idea of what Ramon might look like in twenty-five years—as gorgeous as ever.

"Callie," Ramon said, "I'd like you to meet my dad, Eduardo Cruz. Dad, this Callie Jamison, the friend I told you about."

"Call me Eddie," the dashing older man said with a grin. "My friends do."

"All right, I will." She offered both men a cheery smile. "It's nice to meet you, Eddie."

It was also very nice to know that Ramon still considered her his friend and that he hadn't decided to steer clear of her.

She wondered what he'd told his father about her,

but she shook off her curiosity, reached for the white mug that rested upside down in front of Ramon's place setting and filled it with the fresh morning brew. Then she did the same with Eddie's mug.

"I'm surprised I haven't seen you in town or at the café yet," she said. "Then again, I've only worked here for a couple of months."

Eddie reached for his mug. "I used to come into town more often, but I've been sticking close to the ranch lately."

Was he avoiding Helena? Or waiting for the gossip to die down? Callie wasn't about to ask, but she'd sure like to hear his side of the story.

"Excuse me," Eddie said, as he pushed his chair back from the table and got to his feet. "I see someone I should probably talk to." Then he got up from his seat and walked to the back, clearly heading for Helena's table.

Callie fought the compulsion to watch the scene unfold, hoping it would go a lot smoother than the last time. Instead, she remained focused on Ramon, which wasn't hard to do. Most women wouldn't be able to keep their eyes off him.

"I'll get you a couple of menus," she said.

"We don't need any. My dad wants the waffle special and a bowl of fruit." Ramon's drop-dead smile lit his eyes. "And I'll have oatmeal, an English muffin and orange juice."

"What?" she asked in mock surprise. "You're

not going with the usual? No eggs sunny-side up? No hash browns or bacon?"

He lifted his mug, took a sip of coffee and winked. "I didn't want to mention…" He lifted a cupped hand to his mouth and silently spelled out *B-A-C-O-N*. "I didn't want to send you running to the restroom."

Her cheeks warmed, no doubt turning them a bright shade of pink, yet she couldn't rein in the grin that stretched across her face. "It wasn't just the mention of a bacon cheeseburger that set me off. I'd had a light lunch and was a little overwhelmed after seeing that ultrasound and talking to the doctor."

"I imagine the news would make anyone a little wobbly and nauseous."

"Yeah, well… I'm adjusting." She shrugged a single shoulder. "I'm a little surprised to see you here today."

"Why? I eat a lot of meals here."

"After Friday night, I figured you'd rather drive across town."

"Good eats. Great service. Why burn the gas to go anywhere else?"

She was tempted to thank him for not running scared, but she opted to keep quiet and let it go. "I'd better get your order in."

If only things were different…

Chapter Six

Ramon watched Callie as she turned away from the table and headed toward the kitchen. She hadn't gone far when her steps slowed to a stop. She pulled her cell from her apron pocket, opened the lid and looked at the display.

While it wasn't his business, he wondered whom she was expecting to hear from. Her friend Alana, most likely.

She slipped the phone back into her apron pocket and continued on her way. Her walk had a natural yet enticing sway that stirred his thoughts in a surprisingly sexual way.

You'd think that her pregnancy would've squelched

his physical attraction, but for some damned reason, it hadn't. Not yet, anyway.

As he watched her work, as she saw to the needs of the other diners, he realized there was something maternal about her, something oddly appealing. He wondered why he hadn't noticed before. But then again, he'd pretty much grown up without a mother of his own, so he probably lacked the ability to pick up on stuff like that.

There was something else that drew him to her. A certain vulnerability, he supposed. He'd always had the heart of a rescuer. His dad had pointed it out to him yesterday at the ranch, while they'd saddled the horses. Both men enjoyed riding, although they didn't get a chance to do it often enough. Being outdoors on horseback gave them a chance to talk about stuff, and Callie's name had come up more than once.

That's why his dad suggested they meet for breakfast this morning at the Meadowlark Café. He'd wanted to see what his son found so appealing about the pregnant waitress.

Ramon glanced across the room, to where his dad stood next to Helena's table, talking to her while Marianne looked on, clearly hanging on to every word.

Helena said something, then his father nodded and returned to the table.

"How'd it go?" Ramon asked.

"All right, I guess. Helena feels terrible about that god-awful mess at the Blue Moon Inn. And I told her it was all forgotten. I even said maybe we could go out for a cup of coffee one of these days."

"Seriously?" Ramon found it a little hard to believe his dad would offer an olive branch after all the woman had put him through, not just that night, but when he'd been called to court as a witness.

Dad shrugged. "Helena's actually a nice person. In fact, she rarely drinks, and when she does, she's a real lightweight. She's not prone to being flighty or temperamental. So I know those Long Island Iced Teas hit her hard. Besides, I think my efforts to put that evening behind us might end up putting the gossip to rest."

"People haven't been talking about it as much lately, so I think the story may be dying down, anyway."

"Maybe. For the time being. But folks aren't likely to forget things like that. It's been rough on Helena, especially since she lives in town. I told her not to beat herself up for a night we'd both like to forget."

Was there any wonder why Ramon admired and respected his father? Eduardo Cruz was a good man. The best. He was bright, good-hearted and honest, especially with the women he dated. And he wasn't the type to get embroiled in a small-town scandal.

"I reminded her that I'd always been up front," Dad said. "I don't make long-term commitments and I'm not ever going to get married again."

Ramon couldn't blame him. He'd only been married to Ramon's mom for a few years, and they'd never been especially happy. But she'd always harbored big dreams of being a singer, and one day she ran off with a country band, hoping to kick off the career she'd put off to marry Eduardo. She'd told his father that she wasn't cut out to be a wife and mother. Apparently that was true because they'd never heard from her again.

The front door creaked open, drawing Ramon's attention, as Burl and Thelma Masters entered the café. The older couple must have decided to stop for breakfast either before or after church.

Shannon O'Malley entered the dining room from the kitchen and greeted Burl and Thelma with a cheery, "Good morning, Mr. and Mrs. Masters. Take any seat you want. I'll bring over some coffee to start."

Burl and Thelma chose a table next to Ramon while Shannon grabbed two menus from the counter.

Shannon was a good kid, although her aunt Gloria, the Meadowlark Café's cook, didn't seem to appreciate her zest for life or her sense of style.

After greeting the couple himself, Ramon pointed at Shannon's short-cropped black hair, the spiked tips dyed purple this week. "I see you've been to the salon again."

Her expression lit up. She lifted her hand and fingered the spikes on top. "You like it?"

He tossed her a crooked grin. "Sure do."

"Thanks. Gloria gets all bent out of shape when I get experimental, especially with my hair. But my friend Hailey just graduated from beauty school and got a job at The Mane Event on Second Street. She likes to practice on me. My aunt thinks that's crazy. But hey." Shannon flashed a smile. "I don't mind being Hailey's guinea pig, especially when it's free. Besides, we have fun."

"*Excuse* me," Burl said, his voice slightly raised and laced with annoyance. "Can you *please* get our coffee?"

"Sure thing." Shannon smiled at the man, then winked at Ramon. "I gotta get back to work, but just so you know, Hailey is looking for new clients. If you tell her I sent you, she'll give you a good deal."

"I'll keep that in mind," Ramon said.

Shannon had no more than taken a few steps away when Ramon turned his attention back to his father. But before he could form a single word, Shannon called out, "Whoops," followed by the sound of shattering glass. Shannon dropped an F-bomb as she gazed at the broken carafe lying in a puddle of coffee on the floor, then covered her mouth with a hand as if she could somehow push the word back before the customers or her aunt heard it.

Too late. Gloria swept out of the kitchen, brow furrowed, anger blazing in her eyes. "What's the matter with you, Shannon? Are you trying to get us both fired? That's the third thing you've broken this week."

"I'm sorry, Aunt Gloria."

"Damn," Burl called out. "I hope that's not the only pot you have. I can't get by without my morning coffee."

Ramon was about to step in when Callie made her way toward the mess with a mop, along with a broom and dustpan.

"I've got it," Callie told Gloria. "Go back in the kitchen. We'll have this cleaned up in no time at all."

"Of course you will, Callie. That girl is a screwup, and you're always covering for her."

Dad leaned back in his seat and folded his arms across his chest. "This ought to be interesting. Gloria's one tough cookie. Let's see how your new friend handles her."

Callie handed the broom and dustpan to Shannon, keeping the mop to use herself. All the while, Gloria stood watch over the cleanup efforts, a scowl on her face, hands pressed against her hips.

Gloria might be a talented, hardworking cook,

but they'd all be much better off if she'd stay out of the dining room, especially during Shannon's shifts. As far as Callie was concerned, she was way too hard on her niece. Shannon might be a little ditzy at times, but she was a good kid.

"I've got this," Callie told Gloria. "Why don't you get back to work? I'm sure you've got better things to do."

"Hey!" Burl called out. "Who's getting my coffee?"

Gloria let out a humph, which seemed more directed at her niece than Burl. "I've got another pot brewing in the kitchen. I'll get it for you."

It took all Callie had not to roll her eyes or make a bigger scene than it needed to be. But she wouldn't do that in front of customers. And on top of that, Jasmine Daniels, the owner of the Meadowlark Café, usually showed up on Sunday mornings, and Callie wanted to stay on her good side—for more reasons than the obvious.

Jasmine had mentioned selling the restaurant in the fall, and Callie had already told her she was interested in buying it. She'd love to turn it into a trendy café, using produce from local farmers, as well as meat and dairy products from the ranchers. Fairborn had seen a population boom once classes began at the new junior college, and she thought she could draw in a younger crowd, as well as the regulars. But with twins on the way, everything had changed—and she didn't think she was in any position to risk that kind of investment.

After returning with a fresh coffee carafe, Gloria filled two mugs, one for Burl and the other for Thelma. Then she pointed at Shannon, who'd picked up the broken glass. "You. Me. Now." She nodded toward the kitchen.

"Chill," Callie said. "Accidents happen, and we've almost got this mess cleaned up."

Gloria's eye twitched, but she didn't speak, didn't move.

Callie tore the top sheet off her pad with Ramon's order and handed it to her. "I'll get Burl and Thelma's, then bring it to you."

The fiftysomething cook let out another humph, this one more exaggerated than the other, and strode out of the dining room.

Once the mess was clean and she'd washed her hands, Callie returned to Ramon's table. "Sorry about that."

"No problem. You handled that well." He turned to his father. "Don't you think so?"

"Yep, you put out that fire with grace and a cool head. I've known Gloria for years. She's a hell of a good cook, but she's got an ornery streak and a quick temper."

Before Callie could agree, Ramon's cell phone rang. She hadn't meant to listen in on a personal conversation, but when he furrowed his brow, looked at her and silently mouthed, "It's Mark," she couldn't walk away.

Maybe it was the mother in her, but she'd grown fond of the Johnson boys. And Ramon's expression seemed a little too intense for comfort.

Callie could only hear one side of the conversation, but she tried to figure out what Mark might be saying on the other end.

"I'm sorry to hear that," Ramon said. "Did she call the doctor?"

Uh-oh. Was Jesse sick? Or had he been injured? Why hadn't Katie called herself?

"I know it's Sunday, but the urgent care is open until three o'clock." Ramon raked a hand through his hair. "Okay. I'll come and get you and Jesse. You can stay with me for a while, and that'll give your sister some peace and quiet. She might feel better if she can take a nap."

Ramon glanced at his Apple Watch, then at his uneaten breakfast. "Tell Katie I'll be at your apartment in about twenty minutes. You and Mark can hang out with me until about three thirty. The mayor called an emergency meeting at four, and I can't miss it, so I'll probably have to bring you home on my way to the city hall."

When Ramon disconnected the line, Callie couldn't help but ask, "Is Katie sick?"

"Yeah." Ramon slipped his phone back in his pocket. When he looked up, concern marred his brow. "It sounds like a stomach bug of some kind. I'm going to take the boys so she can get some rest."

"That's sweet of you."

He shrugged, as if uneasy with the compliment. But not many men would volunteer to babysit for a family that wasn't his own, and Callie's admiration for him grew.

Yet so did her concern for the young woman who was pedaling as fast as she could to be both mother and father to her younger brothers. "Is Katie going to see a doctor?"

He slowly shook his head. "She told Mark she didn't need to. And she's probably right. I think she's exhausted after all she's taken on—the boys, work, school."

Callie often worried about Micah doing the same thing, especially when she wasn't around to remind him to eat well and to get his sleep.

"I'm off at three today," she said. "Instead of taking the boys home, drop them off with me. I'll take them to the ranch and they can hang out there. And I'll feed them dinner. That way, Katie can get a full day of rest."

"Will Alana mind having a couple of kids around?" he asked.

"No, she loves children. But she's at a cattle symposium in Colorado and won't be home until tomorrow afternoon."

"All right, then. But my meeting could go into

overtime, so I'm not sure when I'll be able to pick them up."

"No problem. I'll fix dinner for you, too. I don't often get a chance to show off my cooking skills. And if you aren't able to break away from that meeting until late tonight, you can take a plate home with you."

"Sounds good." His gaze zeroed in on her in a way that caused her chest to warm and her heart to rumble. "Thanks, Callie."

"That's what friends are for." She cast him a smile, yet something deep inside stirred in a not-so-friendly way.

Ramon arrived at city hall to attend the emergency, closed-door meeting Mayor Sam Hawkins had called and parked in the lot near Town Square. After grabbing his briefcase and locking his SUV, he walked along the elm tree–shaded sidewalk and headed for the redbrick building that housed city hall and several other government offices.

Once inside, the relatively new receptionist, a blonde in her early forties, greeted him with a professional smile. "Good afternoon, Councilman. The mayor is in the conference room."

"Thanks, Kelly." Ramon continued past the gurgling, Spanish-tiled water fountain created by a local artisan and continued down the long hallway. The door to the dark-paneled room was open.

Mayor Hawkins, who was wrapping up his second term, was seated at the large, solid oak table, his back to a colorful mural of Fairborn's early ranching years. Cynthia Cox, the red-haired, fiftysomething city attorney, sat next to him.

Ramon pulled out a chair directly across from them, just as the other four council members began to trickle in. Once they'd all taken a seat, Cynthia got up and closed the door, securing their privacy.

"What's up?" Jim Crowder, the silver-haired senior member of the council, asked.

The mayor leaned back in his chair, the springs creaking, and sighed. "I'm afraid Bryan Livingston left us with a hell of a parting shot."

Livingston, a former councilman who'd been married more than twenty years, had abused his expense account by using it to pay for business trips that were actually vacation getaways with his lover, who was a secretary at the Department of Public Works. That in itself was bad enough, but thanks to his lover's inside information, he'd been privy to the bids various contractors had made and then provided that info to a competitor willing to pay the price. Fortunately, he'd been convicted of political corruption and fraud, and it was his term Ramon had been appointed to complete.

What had the scoundrel done now?

"You probably don't remember Vickie Tomlinson," Hawkins said. "She worked as a receptionist at city hall up until six months ago, when she quit rather suddenly." The mayor blew out a sigh. "She filed a sexual harassment suit against the city, claiming Bryan made her life miserable while she worked here, and that her complaint wasn't taken seriously."

Ramon leaned forward. "Is that true?"

"Her claim that Bryan acted inappropriately?" the mayor asked. "Probably. I wouldn't put anything past him at this point."

"Neither would I," Ramon said. "But did she actually file a formal complaint? And if so, what happened to it?"

Mayor Hawkins cleared his throat, looked at Cynthia a bit sheepishly, then addressed the others in the room. "I didn't take the proper action. She quit, then Bryan was removed from office, so I figured her accusations were no longer an issue."

"Wrong," Cynthia said. "Now Fairborn is facing a lawsuit, and it looks like we'll have to settle."

No one had to point out the obvious—the town's finances hadn't yet recovered from Bryan's misuse of funds and a slew of lawsuits that continued to roll in.

"What's this going to cost us?" Ramon asked the attorney.

"It's hard to say at this point. She's claiming it caused her to have a nervous breakdown, so it could be upward of a million dollars."

Ramon shot a glance at the retiring mayor. "Why didn't you mention any of this to us?"

"Like I said, I thought it went away." The older man shrugged. "I realize now that I should have."

"Yes, you should have." Crowder chuffed. "Well, I guess we'll just have to cough it up. Do we have enough? What about our insurance?"

Mayor Hawkins scrubbed a hand over his furrowed brow. "No insurance."

Another misstep on the mayor's part.

"We'll have to postpone the plan to refurbish the community center," Ramon said.

"Let me see what, if anything, I can negotiate." Cynthia clicked her ballpoint pen a couple of times, then made a note on her legal pad. "I'm meeting Tomlinson's attorney tomorrow. I'll report back to you as soon as I can."

On that note, the meeting ended.

And so did any hopes of getting the community center back up to code. What century did the mayor live in?

Frustrated and disappointed by the news, Ramon headed to the Lazy M, which was about ten miles out of town. Along the way, he called Katie to check on her.

"I'm feeling a little better," she said. "I slept for a while, but my stomach still hurts."

"Are you able to eat? Do you need anything?"

"I'm not hungry, but I had a piece of toast. And

there's a can of chicken soup in the cupboard. So I'll be okay."

"Good. Take it easy, and don't worry about the boys. I'll bring them home after dinner."

"Thanks, Coach. I really appreciate this. If my mom…" Her voice wobbled, and she paused.

"I know. It's been rough." Ramon had lost his mother—although under completely different circumstances—so he at least had a vague idea as to how lost she must be feeling at the moment.

Katie sniffled. "Sorry."

"You'll get through this. And I'll help out whenever I can."

After they ended the call, Ramon turned onto the graveled drive that led to the Lazy M.

About six months ago, after he and his dad heard that Jack McGee had cancer and wasn't expected to live, they'd gone to visit him, to ask if he needed anything. Jack had always been strong and self-sufficient. So it wasn't surprising when he claimed to be doing okay, even when one look at his failing body claimed otherwise. He also mentioned that he'd been talking to a Realtor about putting the ranch on the market. But then he'd met the granddaughter he hadn't realized he had and left it to her instead.

When Ramon came to take Callie to the Silver Dollar Saloon, he'd noticed that Alana had begun to fix a few things. The front gate had been repaired, although it needed paint. And the lawn in front of the house had been mown, the rose garden weeded. But Jack had been sick a long time, and other than a new roof on one of the outbuildings, the ranch was pretty run-down. There was a lot left for her to do.

At least she didn't have very many cattle to worry about. Jack's herd had dwindled over the past couple of years. Apparently, Alana planned to build it back up again, although he wasn't sure that she'd gain enough know-how by attending a symposium.

He pulled into the front yard and parked near the barn, which could use a new roof, too, as well as a fresh coat of paint. As he climbed from the vehicle, a cattle dog wearing a new red collar trotted out of the open barn door to greet him, its tail wagging.

The Johnson boys followed behind, smiles stretched across their faces, but that wasn't surprising. They lived in an apartment complex in town, so running around on a ranch had to be a new experience for them. And a healthy one.

"We've been playing rodeo," Jesse said. "There are a couple of old saddles on wooden stands in the barn, so we've been sitting on them and pretending to be cowboys."

A grin tugged at Ramon's lips. "That's cool. I'm glad you're having fun."

"Callie's in the kitchen," Mark said. "She's making spaghetti and told us it would be ready in five minutes."

"Yeah," Jesse added. "But I think it's already been longer than that. You gonna to eat with us, Coach?"

"I never turn down a home-cooked meal." Especially if Callie would be eating with him.

"Come on," Jesse said. "I'll show you where we're supposed to wash up."

He followed the boys around to the side of the house, up the wooden porch steps—several of which needed to be replaced—and in the back door.

"Coach is here!" Mark called out as they headed toward the sink in the service porch, which was just off the kitchen.

The warm aromas of basil, tomatoes and garlic filled the air, and it struck Ramon that he hadn't had a home-cooked meal in… Hell, he couldn't even remember. Jillian hadn't liked to cook, so they'd ended up grilling or eating takeout more often than not.

"Perfect timing," Callie called out while he and the boys took turns washing up at the sink in the mudroom. After drying their hands, they entered the kitchen.

"Something sure smells good," Ramon said.

Callie turned from the stove and tossed him a

bright-eyed grin that made him rethink his priorities about home and hearth… Damn. Did he even have priorities these days?

The round oak table had already been set, and a tossed salad in a red bowl sat on the counter near the stove. Still, Ramon asked, "Is there anything I can do to help?"

"Not a thing," Callie said. "All I need to do is pull the bread out of the oven."

Minutes later, they took their seats at the table and began to eat their fill of spaghetti, salad and toasty garlic bread. The boys each had a glass of milk, while the adults drank iced herbal tea, which had a sweet blueberry taste that was surprisingly good and refreshing.

"Everything is delicious," Ramon said. "You're a great cook, Callie. If Jasmine ever decides to fire Gloria, you could take her place."

Callie laughed. "I don't know about that. I do okay when it comes to cooking dinner for a few people, but I'd probably be a hot mess if I had to whip out a variety of different meals for a dining room full of hungry customers. But that doesn't mean I wouldn't give it my best shot."

"Then I'm glad you included me tonight."

Once word had gotten out that Jillian was gone for good, several single women in town had invited Ramon to come over and have a home-cooked meal with them. But he'd known their intentions.

And he wasn't going to jump into another relationship unless he had a damn good reason to believe it would be a meaningful one—for everyone involved. This was the first invitation Ramon had accepted—from his friend Callie.

"I sure wish we lived on a ranch," Jesse said. "If we did, I'd have a horse of my own."

His brother nodded in agreement as he sucked a dangling spaghetti noodle into his mouth.

"Living on a ranch isn't all fun and games," Ramon said. "You'd both have a lot of chores to do."

"We wouldn't care about that," Jesse said. "Not if we had a dog like Rascal and got to go horseback riding."

That was probably true. When Ramon was a kid, he hadn't minded the chores, mostly because his dad used to work along with him.

"Can me and Jesse be excused?" Mark asked. "We'll help with the dishes. We always do at home. But we want to go outside with Rascal for just a little while longer. Before it gets too dark."

"Put your plates and glasses on the counter," Callie said. "And don't worry about the dishes tonight. I'll do them after you leave."

The boys happily thanked Callie, then once they'd left their dishes near the sink, they called Rascal and rushed outside. The dog trotted along behind them, its tail wagging.

When the back door shut, Callie asked, "Have you talked to Katie?"

"Yes, I called her on the drive here. She's feeling better after a nap, but her stomach still hurts."

"If it continues to bother her, she probably ought to see a doctor."

"I'll mention that when I take the boys home." Ramon pushed back his chair and picked up his own plate, as well as Callie's.

"You don't need to do that." She reached out and snatched his wrist, her fingers softly pressing into his skin and sending a rush of heat zip-lining through his veins.

He didn't pull away, didn't want to. And she didn't let go. Something mesmerizing surged between them and their gazes locked, connecting them in a way her grip couldn't.

Thoughts and feelings he hadn't had in a long, long time—if ever—swirled in his brain. Warm, domesticated images.

A man coming home after being away far too long.

The aroma of a tasty meal.

The smile of a pretty woman.

The feeling that he finally had someone behind him, someone who'd always have his back.

Callie released his wrist, scattering his thoughts to the wind and breaking their temporary connection. That was a good thing, right?

"Okay," she said, her voice soft and a bit shy, "I'll let you help."

He carried the plates to the sink, then turned on the water and waited for it to heat. In the meantime, he bent down, opened the cupboard door and reached for the plastic bottle of dish soap.

Moments later, with the sink filled with warm, sudsy water and a yellow dish towel in Callie's hands, Ramon washed a plate, rinsed it and handed it to her. She dried it carefully, making slow, circular motions, then put it away.

She'd been right. It wasn't going to take long to clean up after dinner, especially when they worked together, but Ramon wasn't in a hurry to get things done. Or to drive back to town.

"You're good at this," she said. "You must've washed a lot of dishes when you were a kid."

"I sure did. I had a lot of chores back then— laundry, vacuuming, cleaning bathrooms. Most of the time, my dad worked along with me. But on school nights, he did the chores himself. He let me know that my education was important to him, and that made it important to me, too."

"He was a good parent."

"You're right. I couldn't have asked for a better dad." Ramon rinsed off another plate, then handed it to Callie. "I have a lot of love and respect for him. I always did, but even more so now. We're pretty tight."

"I could see that earlier today. At the café." Callie placed the dried plate into the cupboard. "I'm glad I got to meet him."

"So am I."

"It surprised me to see him talking to Helena," Callie said. "Under the circumstances, that was a kind and gracious thing for him to do. I admire him."

"My dad may be a rancher and a cowboy, but he's got more class than a lot of college professors or Wall Street stockbrokers I've met."

"I don't doubt that."

"For what it's worth, he came away with admiration for you, too." Not that Ramon had asked for his father's opinion. In fact, Eddie hadn't said a word after they left the café to go their own ways. He just smiled and gave Ramon a thumbs-up sign.

That simple motion validated what Ramon already knew—Callie was special. And she'd be a good friend.

As Callie put the last of the clean silverware into the drawer, Ramon rinsed out the sink. Then he wrung out the dishcloth, folded it and draped it over the faucet, something his dad taught him to do.

"I could have cleaned up myself," she said, "but thanks for the help."

He tossed her a playful smile. "I had an ulterior

motive. That was my way of making sure I'd get invited back for dinner someday."

As their gazes met, they locked tight and firm. Something stirred deep inside, urging Ramon to do what he'd been tempted to do all evening. He placed a bent index finger under Callie's chin, lifting her face to his.

Her lips parted, and he kissed her, softly and tentatively, providing time for her to put a halt to it.

But he hoped she wouldn't.

Chapter Seven

Considering the embarrassment she'd felt following their first kiss, Callie had known better than to let it happen again. But the moment Ramon slipped his arms around her and drew her into a warm embrace, she leaned into him, her breasts pressed against his chest.

As she savored his alluring scent, a subtle blend of man, musk and a woodsy aftershave, her willpower circled down a long, bottomless drain.

Her lips parted on their own, and when his tongue swept into her mouth, seeking and finding hers, her knees weakened, and she lost herself in the arousing moment.

She savored his taste, the lingering hint of sweet

blueberries, and couldn't seem to get enough of it. Or of him.

Call her stupid, but she was losing her head over the guy. She just hoped she wouldn't lose her heart.

As their tongues mated, desire shot straight to her core. She wasn't ready to let go of him until a burst of giggles sounded from the doorway, dousing desire like a cold shower.

The kiss ended abruptly, leaving Callie with wobbly knees and a passion-fogged brain.

Ramon stepped to the side to face the boys while she reached for the counter in an attempt to steady herself, catch her breath and gather her wits.

Jesse, the younger brother, chuckled. "Hey, Coach. We caught you."

"You didn't catch anything," Ramon said. "I was just thanking our hostess for an amazing meal."

"With a kiss like that?" Mark laughed. "We watch TV, dude. And we aren't dumb. That wasn't a thank-you kiss. It was the mushy kind guys give their girlfriends."

"I'm sure it probably looked that way," Ramon said. "But it was the friendly kind."

Neither boy appeared convinced. And Callie wasn't sure what to think, either. That kiss hadn't been the least bit friendly, not even at the start. So why did Ramon claim that it had been?

She supposed he didn't want Jesse and Mark to

tell anyone about what they'd just seen. If the other boys on the team found out, the town rumor mill would catch wind of it. So he must be making an attempt at damage control. That made sense, especially for a community leader who hoped to be elected mayor in the fall.

"I'll tell you what." Ramon rubbed his hands together, then clapped them, just like any coach would do after a sports team broke a huddle. "Now that we've eaten and the dishes are done, I'll take you boys home."

"Okay," Jesse said. "It's a school night, and Katie likes us to go to bed early. We already got our homework done, but she makes us shower and set our clothes out and stuff like that."

"Thanks for bringing us to the ranch and for an awesome dinner, Callie." Mark turned to Ramon, his eyes twinkling and a smirk sliding across his face. "I hope it's okay that me and Jesse just *said* thank you to Callie? I mean, I have friends at school who are girls, but I don't kiss them. Not like that."

"Okay, wise guys. Go get in the car."

The brothers hurried outside, giggling and whispering as they went.

Ramon raked a hand through his hair, then he turned to Callie. "I…uh…I'm not sure what to say. I guess… I got a little carried away."

"We both did. But Mark was right. That kiss wasn't the friendly kind."

"I…uh…" He sucked in a breath, then let it out. "You're right. And if you're looking for an apology or an explanation, I'm not sure I can come up with either right now. Can we talk about it later?"

"Sure." But she didn't quite know how she felt about it, either.

He nodded toward the doorway. "I'd better go. And on the way home, I'm going to have a little chat with Jesse and Mark about things like appreciation, loyalty and not spreading gossip."

So she'd been right. He was concerned about his political ambition and his standing in the community. She supposed she couldn't blame him, but it still hurt.

"Thanks again for dinner," he said. "Have a good evening."

"You, too." She followed him to the door, and as he left the house, she locked up for the night.

That so-called friendly kiss had knocked her ever-lovin' socks off, and if the boys hadn't been at the ranch, it might have knocked off more of her clothing than that.

She had no idea what Ramon really had on his mind. All she knew was that she wished things could be different. That kiss had left her longing for more. And she wasn't just talking about sexual longing.

Did he harbor any romantic thoughts about her, too?

Or had that heated kiss been a result of pure lust, a mere rush of testosterone that had gotten out of hand?

Either way, it was going to be a long, quiet night. The only good thing about being in an empty house and going to bed alone was that when she woke up, it would be Monday, and she'd have a chance to talk to Micah.

Then again, that wasn't necessarily an upside. Who knew what her son would say when she told him he was going to be a big brother—times two?

The next morning, a few minutes before the clock on the living room wall struck ten, Callie's cell phone rang. She'd tucked it into the front pocket of her jeans to keep it handy, but when she reached for it, she fumbled a couple of times before she finally pulled it out. When she spotted Micah's name on the display, relief settled over her.

"Hey," she said. "I was just going to call you in case you forgot."

"I remembered, Mom."

They'd been communicating a lot via text, which was better than nothing. But she loved hearing his voice.

"What's up?" he asked.

"I have some news to tell you, honey. And it isn't going to be easy."

"What's wrong?"

"Nothing. But I'm not sure how you'll feel about it."

"All right. I'm listening."

She took a seat on the faux-leather recliner, sucked in a deep breath, then slowly let it out. "Remember this past winter, when I was living in Texas and told you that I was dating Garrett?"

"Yeah. The guy lied to you about being single. And then you broke up with him and moved to Aunt Alana's ranch in Montana. Don't tell me you took him back."

"Absolutely not." Callie bit down on her bottom lip, then pressed on, "It's just that I didn't realize it at the time, and not until I settled in at the ranch and picked up my waitressing job, but I'm pregnant."

When he didn't say a word, she pressed her cell phone against her ear, as if she could squeeze a reaction out of him.

Finally, he said, "You've got to be kidding."

"No."

"Oh wow." More silence. "You're going to have a *baby*?"

She sucked in a deep breath, then softly let it out. "Actually…I just had my first checkup, and I learned that there are going to be two babies. Twins."

"I… Dang, Mom. I don't know what to say."

She'd known he'd be surprised. She just hoped he wouldn't also be angry, resentful…embarrassed. And if so, that those feelings wouldn't last.

He let out a mock chuckle. "And you sat me down before I left for college to have that little birth control speech."

She blew out a sigh. "Yeah. Ironic, isn't it?"

"*I* think so." He cleared his throat, then added, "Don't worry, Mom. I'll go to the admissions office later this afternoon and file an incomplete on my classes—"

"*Absolutely not!* I'm going to be just fine. I have a doctor here in Fairborn who said everything looks good. And Alana was a nanny, remember? She'll help me after the babies are born. So I'm in good hands."

After another long pause, he said, "I didn't have a problem when you told me you'd started dating. You'd dedicated your life to me for years, so I thought it was cool that you'd found someone special, even though he turned out to be a sorry excuse for a man. And speaking of Garrett the jerk, how does he fit into the picture?"

"He doesn't. Not at all." Callie bit down on her bottom lip, waiting for Micah to speak, to reassure her that he was going to be okay with it all. When he didn't respond, she said, "I didn't plan for this to happen. And I was probably more surprised than you are. But I'm beginning to feel good about it. And I hope that with time, you will, too."

"It's going to definitely take time," he said. "I have to admit, it's knocked me off stride."

"Are you angry? Upset?"

"No. Not really. I'll be okay. It's just that I wish you were having someone else's baby. I mean, babies. Someone who deserved to be their dad."

She wished the same thing—that the babies had a different father, one they could grow up knowing, respecting. Loving.

Ramon came to mind, but she shook off the crazy thought as soon as it struck. Sure, he was definitely a much better man than Garrett could ever hope to be, but she couldn't pin her heart on him. Not when he'd never fall in love with her, let alone make a lifetime commitment.

"I'm coming to Montana for a visit," Micah said. "But once finals are over, I'm coming to the ranch to spend the summer with you."

Knowing him as she did, he wasn't thinking about it as a visit, but rather to check on her, to see for himself that she really was going to be all right.

"I know things will be…different," she said. "But you blessed my life in ways I never would have expected. And I'm sure these babies will do the same—for both of us."

"Probably." He paused a moment then said, "I

miss you, Mom. I'm looking forward to seeing you and Aunt Alana in a couple weeks."

"I miss you, too, honey. I can't wait to show you off to my new friends. I'll start shopping around for flights from Dallas to Kalispell, and then I'll email the confirmation with the schedule."

"I know how to book flights," he said. "You have enough to worry about. I mean, manage."

"Okay, honey. I'll let you handle that." *Thank goodness.* She'd been so worried about how he would take the news of her pregnancy, about how it would affect him. He'd been her sole focus for six-teen years—her one and only purpose. And even though he'd matured beyond her wildest imagina-tion, she knew deep down that learning he would no longer be her only child had to sting, at least a little. Yet his supportive words made her feel so proud of the young man she'd raised. And she knew that, no matter what happened, they'd be able to get through this together.

"I'll have to talk to you more about it later," he said. "I've got a study group in thirty minutes, and it's halfway across campus, so I have to run."

Long after the call ended, Callie continued to sit on the sofa, holding her cell phone to her heart. Micah had been completely surprised by the news, which she'd expected. And with a little time to sort things through, he'd probably be okay with it.

As happy as she was to know he'd be visiting

the ranch in a few weeks, that brought up another concern. The kid had an uncanny ability to read her emotions and to pick up on her mood.

Would he figure out that she had feelings for Ramon? That she'd come dangerously close to making another big mistake by caring far too deeply for a man who would never share her same feelings for him?

Either way, she'd better nip her fruitless crush in the bud. She and Ramon might be attracted to each other, but a relationship with him was doomed from the start. And she'd only end up disappointed and hurt when things didn't work out for them in the long run.

Callie spent the rest of the morning and half the afternoon cleaning the kitchen and doing laundry. She seasoned a couple of chicken breasts and placed them in the oven to bake, along with two russet potatoes. While fixing a green salad, she heard the front door open.

"I'm home," Alana called out.

Callie washed and dried her hands, then hurried to the living room, where her friend was placing her suitcase near the brown faux-leather sofa. "How'd the symposium go?"

"All right, I guess."

Micah wasn't the only one who was adept at

reading emotions. And Callie's BFF was clearly troubled about something. "What's wrong?"

Alana rolled her eyes and swore under her breath. "I did something stupid last night." Instead of blurting out whatever she might have done, she reached for her suitcase and then nodded toward the hallway. "I'm going to unpack and take a shower. I might even take a nap. I didn't get much sleep last night."

"Dinner will be ready in about forty-five minutes. Will that give you enough time?"

"Yeah. Sure."

As Alana crossed the room, her steps sluggish, her shoulders slumped, Callie watched her go. She was tempted to tag along behind and ask what had her bothered, but Alana would open up when she was ready.

An hour later, Alana joined Callie at the kitchen table wearing a pair of gray yoga pants and an oversize white T-shirt. She'd swept her dark, curly hair into a messy topknot. Yet she still looked just as pretty as ever. Even wearing a frown.

"It can't be that bad," Callie said.

Alana sat back in her seat and blew out a ragged sigh. "I met a guy in the hotel bar. He was so gorgeous. And you should have seen his suit. I'm talking *expensive*, Cal, and probably tailored just for him. We were both sitting alone, but we kept eyeing each other. After a couple of minutes, he walked over and asked if he could join me."

Callie knew where the story was going, but she kept quiet, waiting for the "something stupid" to come out.

"He bought me a drink. Several, actually. Then we started talking. He had a great sense of humor. And we really hit it off—at least, in a one-night stand way."

"And...?"

"His name is Clay, but I didn't catch his last name, which won't matter. I'm never going to see him again."

"Did you and he...?"

"Yeah." Alana's shoulders slumped. She placed both forearms on the table, leaned forward and looked at Callie as if seeking judgment. But she wasn't going to find any. "He was amazing. It was by far the best sex I've ever had. Not that I've had that much."

Callie was still waiting for the stupid part, because so far, it didn't sound all that bad. "So what happened? Didn't he ask for your number?"

"He might've asked in the morning if I hadn't slipped out of bed and left the room before dawn."

"I take it that means you didn't get his number, either."

"Nope. I didn't see any reason to. We live in different states. And I have a ranch to run. On top of that, he's an attorney and I barely finished high school."

"I hope he wasn't married," Callie said, thinking of Garrett, the lying charmer.

"He wasn't wearing a wedding ring. But I guess he could have taken it off before walking into a bar all alone. Either way, I didn't see a future for us, so I...left."

"You also made sure he'd never find you."

"Yeah, I know."

And that's where the stupid came in. But Callie just kept quiet, letting her friend vent and talk it out.

"Something tells me I just made a big mistake." Alana's gaze sought Callie's as if looking for either validation or disagreement or...something only a BFF could offer. "Did I?"

"I wouldn't say that."

"What *would* you say, Cal?"

"That you had great sex last night with an amazing guy named Clay. And he left you with a bittersweet memory you'll never forget."

Alana sat up and smiled. "I love you, Cal. You always know how to make me feel better."

"That's what friends are for."

"Ain't that the truth." Alana blew out a sigh. "You have no idea how much I appreciate you. You've been going to bat for me ever since you begged your aunt to let me move in with you guys."

How could she not? Alana had just aged out of foster care. She'd had nowhere else to turn.

"You've always been there for me, too," Callie said. "When Derek died, you sat up with me all night long, holding me when I cried. And you stood by my side at the funeral."

Callie had only been fifteen at the time, and Derek had been two years older. But she'd loved the brilliant teen with a wild, yet boyish side that had appealed to her sweet, obedient nature. And she'd been devastated when he died in a crash while racing another motorcyclist.

She closed her eyes and tried to envision Micah's father, yet try as she might, his image faded a little more each day until it was just a hazy blur. She didn't even have a yearbook picture of him.

Callie smiled wistfully. "I don't think I could have made it through my grief if it hadn't been for you." Not to mention a pregnancy and delivery. Alana had been her birth coach.

"Your aunt might have taken you in and let me stay with you guys, but she wasn't very affectionate or supportive. So I tried to pick up the slack."

"You're right about that. Aunt Rhonda criticized me a lot. I was actually surprised when I found out she'd left her house to me."

"And I ended up with a ranch. Who would have guessed that two teenagers who'd had childhoods as crappy as ours would eventually come out on top?"

Callie smiled. "We've come a long way."

"You can say that again. And just so you know, I'm proud of the woman I've become. I just wish I'd made some better choices when it came to sexual relationships, especially the first one. Thanks to him, I'll never have kids."

When Alana was a senior, one of the high school jocks had bet his friends that he could score with the pretty new girl at school—a foster kid who'd just moved to town. He'd zeroed in on her vulnerability like a lion on the weakest gazelle in the herd. Then, when she'd told him she was going to have a baby, he dropped her like a fumbled football.

After summer, he went off to college without a care in the world. That same year, Alana had lost out on an academic scholarship, then lost the baby.

It broke Alana's heart to know she'd never have a child. And it broke Callie's, too.

Alana's cell phone rang, and she reached into her purse to retrieve it. Then she rolled her eyes. "It's Adam Hastings, that Texas rancher who wants to buy the Lazy M." She slid her finger across the iPhone screen and answered. "Hello, Mr. Hastings. What can I do for you?" She paused. "No, I haven't changed my mind. The Lazy M isn't for sale."

Callie sat forward, eager to hear her friend's side of the conversation.

"That's a very generous offer, but I'm not going to accept it…Uh-huh. I understand that. But tell me, why are you so gung ho on purchasing a property that's not for sale—and paying more than it's worth?"

Alana listened intently, then ended the call. She shot a somewhat stupefied glance at Callie. "I can't believe this. The guy's like a pit bull. He won't take no for an answer, and do you know what he just said to me?"

Callie shook her head.

"I mean, the price he's willing to pay, which I'm pretty sure is about ten percent over its value, is one thing. But then he told me that he's seen the ranch and that he's done his homework. He claims I don't have the money to get it up and running again. And then he said I'd be smart to sell it to him. That way, I can buy myself a nice house in town, which would still leave me with enough money to get a new car and wardrobe."

"What a jerk."

"I don't care if he doubles the offer, Cal. I'm not selling—especially not to him. He's not the only one who assumes Grandpa Jack left me with a slew of financial problems, but I don't care. I've never had a place of my own, never knew a living family member, nor did I expect an inheritance. As far as I'm concerned, I've got a gold mine here."

Before Callie could reply, her own phone rang.

She almost let the call roll over to voice mail, then changed her mind at the last minute and answered quickly, without checking the display.

"Hello?"

"Callie, it's Ramon."

That was a surprise. A nice one. "Hi."

"I…uh. Can I ask you to do me a favor? A big one. But it should only take a few minutes of your time."

She heard the reluctance in his voice, yet she'd do what she could to help him out. "What do you need?"

"Katie is in the ER, and they're talking appendicitis."

"Oh no," she said. "The poor girl."

"I'm with her now. And so are the boys. I told her I'd take them home and keep them while she's in the hospital. For the most part, I can shuffle my schedule around so I can drop them off and pick them up at school. But I have a meeting at five o'clock tomorrow. It's with a political consultant, and he's only in the area that day. I'd normally ask my dad to help out, but he's out of town and not due home until Thursday, so…"

"I'd be happy to watch the boys. Do you want to drop them off at the café? I'm working until four tomorrow."

"That would be awesome. I hated to ask you, but…"

"Hey. That's what friends are for."

"And you're the best," Ramon said.

A smile stretched across her face. He was proving to be a good one, too.

"By the way," Ramon said, "the boys are pretty worried about Katie, especially after all they went through when their mom died."

"I'm sure they are. Poor kids. Would it be okay if I took them to visit her at the hospital when I get off work tomorrow? Katie and I haven't officially met yet, but I'd be happy to help her out with the boys while she's recovering, too. And she'd probably like a chance to get to know me first."

"I'm sure you're right," Ramon said. "How is it that you're always aware of what someone needs before they even ask?"

Maternal instinct, she supposed. But it was also a part of her nature. "I guess you could call it a gift."

"My hat's off to you and to your gift," he said. "Or should I say gifts?"

Her heart warmed at his praise, his appreciation. "I'll see you and the boys tomorrow."

Once the call ended, Alana said, "What was that all about?"

Callie told her about Jesse and Mark, about them living with their half sister who was doing her best to take care of them while going to college and working two jobs.

"Ramon is their baseball coach," Callie added. "He's the one who introduced me to them. They're cool little boys. When you meet them, you're really going to like them."

"I'm sure I will." Alana's smile seemed to wash away her concerns about the "mistake" she'd made. "That little family is lucky to have Ramon in their lives."

True. The guy had proven to be more than just a good coach. A lot more. He'd become a family friend to them and a mentor, too.

Her admiration for him continued to grow, which might lead to her making her own stupid mistake. Because if she allowed her feelings for Ramon to grow any stronger, it would prove to be a big one. And heartbreak was the last thing she needed to deal with while creating a loving home for two babies.

Chapter Eight

The Johnson brothers usually rode the bus home, and their apartment complex was one of the last stops. Since Ramon didn't have a lot of time to waste, he picked them up at Fairborn Elementary. Fortunately, Katie had contacted the school last week and gave her permission for him to pick up the boys and take them to baseball practice. So this wasn't the first time he'd shown up to get them. And it wouldn't be the last.

He waited near a group of parents who seemed to know each other. When the bell rang, several teachers led their classes to the front of the school, where the buses were parked.

Mark was the first to spot Ramon, and he dashed toward him, his brow furrowed. "Hey, Coach. How's Katie? When is she going to get out of the hospital?"

"She came through her surgery fine, but she'll be in the hospital for a while. I'll fill you guys in when we get into the car. Where's your brother?"

"He'll be coming in a minute or two."

Before Ramon could say more, Jesse joined them.

"What's up?" the younger boy asked.

"Let's head to my car, and I'll explain on the way." As the brothers fell into step and followed Ramon to his SUV, he told them what he'd learned from the surgeon earlier today. He shot a glance at Jesse, the younger boy, who seemed to be the most sensitive.

He paled, and his bottom lip quivered. "Is she going to die? Like Mom?"

"No," Ramon said. "She'll be okay."

"But her 'pendix burst," Mark said, his fearful gaze locked on Ramon, begging for reassurance. "That's bad, right?"

It certainly could be, but the surgeon had put Ramon's mind at ease. At least, somewhat. "The doctor said she'll be fine, but she's going to need to spend some time in the hospital. I'll take you to see her as soon as she's allowed to have visitors."

He couldn't blame them for being worried.

Their father had died in a work-related accident when they were in preschool, and then their mom had battled cancer for a couple of years before passing away last spring. If anything happened to Katie, they'd be lost and alone.

"Your sister is in good hands," Ramon said. "The doctors and nurses know what they're doing. So don't worry about her. She'll be home soon, and then watch out. She'll be making you do your homework and clean your rooms before you know it."

Using the key remote, he unlocked the doors, then opened the tailgate and waited for the boys to toss in their backpacks. Then they all climbed into the vehicle.

As they drove to the Meadowlark Café, he glanced in the rearview mirror at the boys. They were usually pretty chatty, but they were as quiet as a couple of wide-eyed possums today. He figured they believed him when he'd told them their lives would be back to normal soon. But clearly, he hadn't eased their minds. Not completely.

"I'll ask Callie to get you guys a couple of great big ice-cream sundaes," Ramon said, hoping to lighten their mood. But they still didn't have much to say on the drive.

He tried to make small talk, and while the boys answered any questions he asked, they remained quiet and pensive, their thoughts clearly on their older sister.

Once they arrived, Ramon opened the front door for them. Even the glass case that displayed the available desserts didn't seem to interest them. But when Callie approached them, her blue eyes bright, their moods finally lightened a bit.

"Hey, guys," she said. "I'll be off in a little while. I hope you don't mind hanging out with me until then."

Both boys nodded, but they didn't show their usual enthusiasm.

She placed a gentle hand on Jesse's head and smiled softly, as if she knew their fear, as if she'd do her best to ease their minds. "If you take a seat in the empty corner booth, I'll get you both ice-cream sundaes. And by the time you finish them, I'll be off the clock."

"Okay." Mark nudged his brother. "Come on, let's go sit down."

When they were out of earshot, Callie turned her attention to Ramon. "Those poor boys. How's Katie doing?"

"She's out of surgery but probably still in recovery. I was able to talk to the surgeon since she listed me as her next of kin. Her appendix burst, so she's going to have to stay in the hospital a week or more."

"Oh no. That's serious."

"It is. But the doctor expects her to pull through without a hitch. I planned to take the boys to visit her this evening, but my meeting could go into overtime. I'm afraid I'll have to have to put it off until tomorrow, after they get out of school." He'd also promised his dad to stop by the ranch and check on the new hired hand.

"I can take them when I get off work," Callie said.

Ramon appreciated the offer, especially with all he had going on today. Hell, the rest of the week didn't look much better.

"You wouldn't mind?" he asked.

She looked up at him and smiled, her expression sweet. Disarming. "No. I don't mind at all."

"I hate to ask you to go out of your way, but the boys are really worried about her, and it might make them feel better to see her for themselves. She's probably concerned about them, too."

"I'm sure she is. We'll make it a quick visit, then I'll take the boys to get a bite to eat. Maybe we can see a movie. What time do you think your meeting will be over?"

"I should be able to pick them up in a couple of hours. Seven o'clock at the latest." Ramon reached out and placed his hand on Callie's shoulder. "Thank you. You're amazing. I have a lot on this week. You have no idea how much I appreciate this."

She tossed him a dazzling smile that damn near turned his heart on edge. "Go do what you have to do. You have my number. Just send a text letting me know where you want to meet and when."

"Will do." Unable to help himself, he bent and kissed her cheek. It wasn't exactly what anyone would call a PDA, but it held a lot more affection than she'd ever know.

Hopefully, the early-bird diners hadn't picked up on it. All his upcoming campaign needed was for any unfounded rumors to get out…no matter how founded they might be.

As soon as Callie's shift ended, she called the hospital to see if Katie was out of recovery and, if so, to ask if she wanted the boys to stop by. Then, after hearing a brief visit would be all right, she drove Mark and Jesse to the medical center to see their sister.

"I hate hospitals," Jesse said as they walked into the lobby.

Callie placed a gentle hand on his small shoulder. "They can be scary places at times, but they can also be happy places. Like when babies are born. And when sick people like Katie get the help they need."

After they stopped by the reception desk to get Katie's room number, she tried to prepare the boys for what they might see. "Katie's just had surgery, so she's going to be groggy from the medication they gave her. Don't expect her to be bright-eyed and bushy-tailed. She'll be pretty tired, too. But each day she'll look and feel better."

"I don't care what she looks like," Mark said. "I just want to tell her I love her. And I want her to come home as soon as she can."

Aw. What a great kid. "She'll like hearing you say that. And since we don't want to tire her out, we won't stay very long."

Their footsteps clicked along the tile floor as they made their way to Katie's room. When they were just a few feet away, Callie slowed to a stop and turned to both boys. "Why don't you guys wait right here. I'll go in first and make sure that she's awake and ready for company."

They nodded their agreement, then Callie slowly entered the room, where a petite brunette lay in bed, tethered to a couple of IV poles and various machines.

Had she been wrong to bring the boys here so soon? Would it upset them to see their sister like that—and in a "scary" place?

Katie turned her head toward the door, her dark hair scraggly, her face pale, her brown eyes dulled by pain and medication. Callie introduced herself.

"I heard about you," Katie said. "The day Jesse got hurt. You made Mark feel better. And you gave him ice cream."

Callie smiled. "I'm glad I could help. The boys have been worried about you, so if it's okay with you, they'd like to see you for a minute or two."

"Where are they?"

"Just outside the room." Callie nodded toward the door. "Ramon dropped them off with me at the Meadowlark Café for a little bit, and they had some ice cream. I told them I'd bring them by to say hello. They know we aren't going to stay very long."

"Thanks. I'm sure they're worried."

Moments later, after Callie waved them in, Mark and Jesse hesitantly entered the room, teary-eyed and clearly concerned.

Katie, who had to feel terrible, managed to put on a brave and healthy front. "Hey, you two. What's up?"

"Are you going to be okay?" Mark asked. "I mean, Coach said you would be. But you look kind of…bad. And sick."

"I know," Katie said. "But I'm feeling better already."

Callie didn't buy it. And by the look on the boys' faces, they were skeptical, too.

"You better be good for Coach and Callie," Katie said.

"We will." Mark nudged Jesse with his elbow. "Won't we?"

Jesse nodded. "When can you go home?"

"It'll be a little while. I'm not sure." Katie shifted her hips, as if trying to get comfortable, then grimaced.

"Does it hurt?" Mark asked.

"A little. But they give me medicine for that. And it's about time for me to have a little more." She closed her eyes tight, then opened them and managed a frail smile. "I know I must look like heck. But don't worry. I'll be home before you know it."

"We probably ought to let you sleep," Callie said.

"Yeah. I'm a little tired. Thanks for bringing them to see me."

"Anytime," Callie said. "They're awesome kids. I'd be happy to help Ramon look after them while you recover. In fact, they can spend a night or two with me at the Lazy M. That is, if you don't mind. We have plenty of room."

"That's a nice offer," Katie said. "Ramon speaks highly of you, so I guess that'll be okay."

After they said their goodbyes, Callie ushered the boys out the door and down the corridor. As they reached the elevator, her phone dinged with a text message. She pulled out her cell and checked.

My meeting was postponed until tomorrow. Where are you guys?

Callie typed out, We just saw Katie. Where do you want to meet?

I'm only 5 minutes away. I'll meet you in the lobby.

She told him okay.

They'd barely taken a seat when he walked through the door, as handsome as ever in a pair of dark slacks and a white shirt, open at the collar.

They boys hurried to meet him. Callie had half a notion to join them, but she stood back, still unsure how to greet a man who was fast becoming more than a friend.

"Katie looks super sick," Jesse said. "But she said she's feeling better and is going to come home as soon as she can."

"I told you she's going to be okay." Ramon ruffled Jesse's hair. Then he looked at Callie. "Thanks for helping me out. And bringing them here."

She smiled. "No problem. I'd be happy to keep them anytime."

"Yeah," Mark said. "She even invited us out to the ranch to stay with her."

Ramon zeroed in on Callie. "You don't mind? I'm going to have a late night tomorrow."

"That's fine."

"Are you sure it'll be okay with Alana?" he asked.

"She loves kids. Besides, I have the next two days off, and we have a spare bedroom with twin beds."

"Good. Then I'll drop them off after school." He nodded toward the lobby door. "Come on. We'll walk you to your car."

As they exited the hospital side by side, she again felt like she'd become a part of a team. It was a nice feeling, one she could get used to. When her shoulder brushed his arm, she felt compelled to slip her hand in his. But she knew better than that. They might be a team for now, but it was sure to be a losing season—and one that would end before too long.

On Friday, Ramon picked the boys up from school and drove them to the Lazy M, where they would spend the night with Callie. He parked next to Callie's car. Before he could shut off the ignition, Rascal the cattle dog rushed around the corner of the barn, barking up a storm.

"Rascal!" Mark called out, finally perking up. "We're back."

"Coach," Jesse said, "can we go play with him?"

"I'm okay with that. But let's say hello to Callie first. Get your backpacks. I'll grab your overnight bag and take it to the house."

The boys hurried out of the Expedition, stopping long enough to greet Rascal, then they headed to the wraparound porch with the dog trotting along beside them, its tail wagging.

Ramon climbed the steps, joining them at the front door, and rang the bell. He expected Callie to answer, but instead it was an attractive brunette who greeted them with an I'm-so-glad-you're-finally-here grin.

"Hey, there." A smile dimpled her cheeks and put a sparkle in her big green eyes as she greeted them, focusing her attention on Mark and Jesse. "I'm Alana. Callie and I are so excited you're going to spend the night here. Come on in."

As the boys stepped into the living room, Alana reached out to shake Ramon's hand with a firm, work-roughed grip. "We haven't met, but I've heard about you. And I've seen your picture in the newspaper. I'm Alana Perez, Jack McGee's granddaughter. Callie's making up the beds in the guest room. She'll be out shortly."

"Ramon Cruz," he said. "Thanks for letting the boys stay with you."

"No problem." She returned her gaze to the boys. "Okay, you guys. I know your names, but tell me who's who."

"I'm Mark," the older boy said. He poked a thumb at his brother. "And that's Jesse. We've been here before. We really like your ranch."

"It's a cool place, isn't it? And it's going to be even better once Callie and I are done fixing it up."

No doubt, Ramon thought. They might be calling it Rancho Esperanza, but it was going to take more than hope and dreams to renovate the Lazy M. And with all that work done by two inexperienced women on a limited budget? That was one hell of a daunting project.

"Callie," Alana called out. "We've got company!"

Mark reached down and gave Rascal a pat on the head. "We really like your dog, too."

"Isn't he great? He came with the ranch."

Ramon scanned the living room, with its scarred hardwood flooring and stone fireplace, its faux-leather furniture. He caught a warm, sweet, buttery whiff of sugar and cinnamon. "Something sure smells good."

"Thanks. I just whipped up a batch of cookies." Alana nodded toward the kitchen. "You're in luck, boys. I doubled the recipe. I hope you like snickerdoodles."

Jesse scrunched his face. "What's that?"

Alana's jaw dropped, and her eyes widened in exaggerated surprise. "You mean you've never had one of the best cookies *ever*?"

"No, but I'd like to try one."

"Good. Most kids are hungry and ready for a snack when they get home from school." She pointed to their backpacks. "Do you have homework? I think it's a good idea to get it done first, then you'll have the rest of the day and night to play and have fun."

"When do we get to try those cookies?" Jesse asked.

Alana chuckled. "Right now. It's always easier to think when you're drinking milk and munching on snickerdoodles."

Mark brightened. "Cool."

"Then come with me." Alana turned toward the kitchen. "After we have a snack and get that work done, I'll take you on a tour of the ranch. It's a bit of a hike, but I think you'll enjoy it."

Both boys lit up as they followed Alana to the kitchen. Ramon wasn't sure if he should tag along with them or not, but when Callie entered the living room, her golden-brown hair pulled back in a ponytail and wearing a breezy smile, he was glad he'd stayed behind.

"I have a pretty tight schedule during the days," he said, "but I can take them to my house in the evenings. I asked my dad if they could stay on the Double C, but he doesn't get home until tomorrow. Then he's taking off on a weeklong fishing trip with an old Army buddy. I don't expect you to take them longer than tonight, so I'll—"

Callie reached out and caught his forearm, her grip tight. "They can stay here as long as they need to. I don't mind running them back and forth to school, since I'm usually working at the café. And when you've got a late meeting, they can stay here."

Her offer went above and beyond, but any help she could provide would certainly help him out, especially this week.

"If you don't mind keeping them," he said, "I'm sure they'd like that. Their moods lightened up the moment we arrived. But shouldn't you run it by Alana first?"

"I don't have to. Alana has a real heart for children."

"From nanny to rancher." Ramon smiled. "I'd call that a big life change."

"It was. But she's happy."

"She certainly seems to be. She welcomed the boys with open arms." Yet he knew it had to be a struggle at times for the two women to make ends meet, so having the boys would probably put a strain on the ranch finances, even if Callie hadn't mentioned it. So he'd make sure to help out. It was the least he could do.

"I really appreciate you and Alana letting Mark and Jesse stay," Ramon said.

"And I appreciate *you*." She blessed him with a heartfelt smile. "You've stepped up to help out their family. Not many men would do that."

Her praise not only pleased him, but it soothed the sense of failure he'd been feeling since his marriage ended. So much so that he felt compelled to stand here and soak it in, but he had a meeting to attend and didn't want to be late.

"I'd better get on the road. I have a lot to do, and I want to stop by the hospital later this evening to check on Katie before visiting hours end."

"Let me know how she's doing," Callie said. "And tell her not to worry about the boys."

"I will. Thanks again."

As Ramon turned to go, Callie reached for his

arm and stopped him. "You know, Katie's going to need help while she recovers. The boys will be in school, and you work during the day. Tell her that, after she's discharged, she and the boys are welcome to stay here for a few days—or as long as she needs to."

The generosity and kindness of the offer, while not unexpected, touched him deeply. He gazed into her pretty blue eyes, damn near drowning in them. Where had this amazing woman been all his life?

"You're something else," he said.

Her cheeks flushed, and she waved him off. "I'm not special. It's just who I am. And what I do."

She was right, he supposed. She always thought of others, whether working at the Meadowlark Café or offering to look after two young boys at the ranch.

A growing compulsion to take her in his arms and kiss her built to the point where it was hard to ignore.

But allowing his hormones to have their way would be stupid. They'd just gotten past that last kiss.

Or had they?

His testosterone surged, and pheromones lit up the air around them. Unable to help himself, he cupped her jaw and caressed her cheek with his thumb. And when she gazed into his eyes, he was toast.

Chapter Nine

Ramon stroked his thumb across Callie's cheek, sending a spiral of heat to her core. As his warm brown eyes zeroed in on hers, he didn't need to utter a single word.

Her lips parted as desire filled her to the brim. But common sense, for once, kept her grounded. She took a step back. "That's not a good idea."

"You're probably right." A slow grin stretched across his face, and his eyes glimmered. "But I can't seem to think of a better one."

Deflecting the starry-eyed moment with humor? That worked for her, so she returned his smile. "I can come up with several. One of which is the boys. They could find you kissing me again, and what would they think?"

"Good point. I guess."

Making light of the situation seemed to set everything to right again—whatever *right* was.

Yet in spite of the humor and taking a step back, Callie's hormones remained on high alert, and even though he'd dropped his hand to his side, her cheek continued to tingle at his touch.

"You know," he said, "we're going to have to talk about this at some point."

"You're right. But not today." And not when she wasn't entirely sure what "this" was—or what it should be. "You have a meeting to attend, remember? And a hospital visit after that. And I have to make a grocery run." She nodded toward the door. "Come on. I'll walk you out."

As they stepped onto the front porch, a bird chirped in the shade of the elm tree in the yard, where it had made a nest. It was a nice reminder of spring, of new life. And setting priorities.

She needed to focus on creating a home for her babies—not on an attraction that had nowhere to go but south.

As Ramon walked with her along the pathway that led to their parked vehicles, he asked, "Do you need anything? Money for those groceries or… whatever?"

Money was always an issue, but she'd never

liked to rely on charity. She'd had to do so too often in the past.

"Thanks for offering," she said, "but we'll be okay. I'm pretty good at planning and stretching meals. And we keep a well-stocked pantry. But we need milk, and I'd better pick up some kid-friendly staples like peanut butter and jelly."

Instead of heading to his SUV, Ramon continued to walk with her to her car. She stole a glance at him and caught him looking at her with… admiration. As if she were…what? Some kind of saint? A princess? She wasn't sure what he imagined her to be, but she was neither.

As he eased closer, she caught a hint of his woodsy scent, which only served to stir up the feelings she'd had moments earlier, feelings she'd tamped down.

Was he going to try to kiss her again?

His arm slipped around her, but instead of drawing her into an embrace, he used his free hand to open the car door. A gallant gesture. And just one more thing to add to the list of qualities she admired in him.

"Drive carefully," he said.

"You, too."

He turned and walked away. Instead of starting the engine, she took a moment to watch the tall, dark and gorgeous hunk saunter toward his SUV.

She couldn't help thinking that he was a bit of a saint himself. And a prince among men.

Yet in spite of her admiration for him and the strong friendship they'd developed, regret filled her heart. And not just because a relationship with him was doomed from the start.

What a dope she'd been. She should have kissed him while she'd had the chance.

While Alana looked after the kids, Callie drove to Tip Top Market, a mom-and-pop-style grocery store that catered to the ranchers and those living outside city limits. Their prices were higher than the supermarket in town, but sometimes it was a lot more convenient to shop there. It was also a great place to catch up on local news.

Ralph and Carlene Tipton had lived in the Fairborn area all their lives, and since they were closing in on retirement age, they knew just about everyone. But shortly after Callie moved to the ranch, Alana had given her a heads-up about them.

Ralph and Carlene are good people. But from what my grandfather said, they may be friendly and good listeners, but they're also prone to gossip. So if you'd prefer not to have your comments printed in the social section of the Fairborn Gazette, *you'd better be careful about how much you share.*

Callie grabbed a red grocery cart from the front

of the store, placed two blue recyclable bags she'd brought from home in the basket and pushed it inside. She would have asked the boys about what kinds of food they liked, but she hadn't wanted to bother them while they were doing their homework.

As she made her way up and down the aisles, she picked out several boxes of macaroni and cheese, a package of hot dogs, a frozen pizza, breakfast cereal, not to mention ketchup, peanut butter and a jar of grape jelly. She also stopped in the produce section to pick out apples, bananas, grapes and some kid-friendly veggies.

"Well, now," Carlene said, as she rang up each item, "it looks like you girls have company out at the Lazy M. I'll bet it's someone who has children."

Callie couldn't see any reason to pretend otherwise. "We'll have a couple of kids visiting over the next week or so."

"Anyone I know?" Carlene asked.

"It's not likely." Callie reached into her purse and pulled out her wallet, hoping the nice but chatty woman would take the hint and finish totaling up the bill.

"Rumor has it you and Ramon Cruz are dating," Carlene added.

"We're good friends. That's all." Callie reached into the bottom of her cart, pulled out the blue sacks and began to bag her own purchase, hoping to move things along.

"He's a good-looking man," Carlene said. "And he and his father own a big ranch about five miles from here. He'd be a good catch."

As if Callie didn't know that. She also knew he'd be a good catch for someone else.

"How much do I owe you?" she asked.

"Sixty-two dollars and fourteen cents."

Callie used her ATM card to pay, then carried her purchases to the car and made the short drive home. A half mile down the road, she spotted the line of mailboxes near the entrance and turned into the ranch. She'd barely gone a hundred yards when she noticed Alana and the boys walking away from the road and toward the house. Alana held a couple of envelopes and some kind of flyer and chatted with Mark and Jesse while Rascal trotted beside them. So did another dog, its scraggly brown fur dirty, its paws muddy.

Callie pulled up beside them and rolled down the passenger window. "What're you guys doing?"

"We went to get the mail," Mark said.

"I can see that. Where'd you find that dog?"

Alana glanced down at the scraggly mutt, then looked up and grinned. "Someone must have dumped him off along the road, thinking he'd get a good home at a ranch. He doesn't have a collar, but he's friendly."

"And in need of a bath," Callie said.

"No problem." Mark stood tall and puffed out his chest in a manly, I-got-this gesture. "Me and Jesse can give him one. We used to have a dog before we moved to the apartment, but we had to give him to our old neighbors."

Callie nearly cringed at the thought. The poor kids had lost their pet, too? No wonder they'd grown attached to Rascal. And now they'd just befriended a stray.

Callie had a pretty good idea what her friend's answer would be, but she asked the question, anyway. "So, what're you going to do with the dog, Alana?"

"I couldn't just leave him wandering on the side of the county road. He might get hit by a car. So, first we're going to feed him, and then we're going to give him that bath."

It was easy to see where this was going. "Do you plan to keep him?"

Alana gave a little shrug, but her lips quirked in a smile and her eyes glimmered. "The boys want to, and since they aren't allowed to have pets at their complex in town, I told them he could stay here."

"He looks like a little Chewbacca," Mark said, "so we're gonna call him Chewie."

"You know," Callie said, "Chewie might have a microchip."

"He might," Alana said. "And I explained that to the boys. I'll schedule an appointment with the vet tomorrow. While we're there, I'll ask if he has one. But in the meantime, Chewie won't have to scavenge for food or a warm, dry place to sleep."

Callie slowly shook her head, and a smile tugged at her lips. There was no one in the world more loving and accepting than Alana, especially when it came to people who were down on their luck. She even had a heart for dogs.

Alana had faced a lot of struggles during her childhood. And as an adult, she'd had a couple of bad breaks. All that she'd been through could make a person angry and bitter, but on Alana, it'd had the opposite effect.

She'd appreciated every single bit of kindness she'd been shown, and now she seemed determined to pay it forward.

"Do you guys want a ride back to the house?" Callie asked.

"No," Mark said. "I mean, me and Jesse don't. We want to walk with the dogs."

Alana placed a hand on Mark's head and gave his hair an affectionate ruffle. "And I want to walk with *you*."

"Then I'll see you at the house."

As Callie continued to drive along the graveled road, her thoughts remained on Alana's loving heart. Alana had always wanted to have a family and a home of her own, a dream that had always seemed to be just out of reach. In a way, she was creating that dream for herself, here on the ranch.

Of course, Mark and Jesse were just spending the night, but Alana didn't care if they stayed a couple of days or weeks. And if Katie came to recover here after being discharged from the hospital, their temporary family would grow. Then Micah would arrive for a visit.

Callie placed her hand on her growing belly. Before they knew it, she'd be bringing her two little ones home to Rancho Esperanza.

Do you need anything? Ramon had asked. *Money for those groceries...or whatever?*

Thanks for offering, but we'll be okay.

But would they?

Her stomach clenched, and she bit down on her bottom lip. Jack McGee's money would run out soon. And if Callie were to have any pregnancy complications, which was possible with twins, she'd be unable to work and would have to tap into her small savings, which was earmarked for emergencies.

She wasn't especially worried about providing for herself and the babies, but Alana would never turn away anyone—or any critter—in need.

And neither would Callie.

But the last thing she wanted to do was to rely on Ramon for help, especially financial. It was bad enough to think she'd never be more than his friend, even if she wished that wasn't the case.

Like it or not, it was just a matter of time before reality kicked in and he realized that she'd be a major complication in a bachelor's life.

If she allowed him to help out financially, where would that leave her?

She'd have to deal with the fact that she and Ramon would never be more than friends. But it would be a whole lot worse if Ramon considered her a charity case.

Chapter Ten

As much as Ramon had wanted to kiss Callie at the ranch, and in spite of his reluctance to hit the road, he'd managed to get back in town before five o'clock, when the county offices would close for the day.

He just hoped that he'd have enough time to get the answers he was looking for. He left his vehicle in the parking lot between city hall and the building that housed the tax collector's office, where Ben Yeager ran the front desk.

Ben and Ramon's dad had been friends since high school, and Ramon knew the man would do whatever he could to provide him with the answers to his question.

Moments later, Ramon opened the door and entered the spacious office.

Ben, a bulky man in his early fifties, looked up from his desk and smiled. "Well, I'll be damned. Look who's here. Fairborn's future mayor."

"I don't know about that, Ben. The election is still months away. It's still anyone's guess how those votes will stack up." Ramon tossed the older man a grin. "How're you doing?"

"I can't complain." Ben got to his feet and met Ramon at the counter. "How's your old man?"

"Couldn't be better. In fact, he's going on a weeklong fishing trip with an old Army buddy."

"Good for him," Ben said. "So what brings you here?"

"A friend of a friend recently inherited the Lazy M Ranch. I know Jack McGee had been sick for a while, and I'd heard he'd gotten behind on a lot of things. Can you tell me if the property taxes are delinquent?"

"Sure can," Ben said. "That's all public knowledge. But there's no need for me to look it up. Jack did get behind, but he made a payment last October, a couple of months before he passed. And then Alana Perez, his granddaughter and the new owner, made another installment three months ago. She's still delinquent, but it looks like she's trying to catch up."

"Wow," Ramon said. "I had no idea you'd have

such a good memory. I thought you'd have to search your records."

Ben folded his arms across his burly chest. "I'd like to take credit for having a superior memory, but I can't. To be honest, you weren't the only one asking about liens and past-due taxes on the Lazy M."

Ramon stiffened and furrowed his brow. "Oh yeah? Who beat me here?"

"An investigator working for a Texas rancher. Some big shot down in Texas. His name's Adam Hastings. You ever hear of him?"

"No, I'm afraid not." Apparently, Ramon would have to do a little investigating of his own. "How much does Alana owe?"

"Close to ten grand—more or less."

Something told Ramon that Alana, even with Callie's help, wouldn't be able to scrape together that kind of money.

"And just so you know," Ben added, "I didn't tell the investigator this, but she hasn't made the second installment of this year's tax payment yet."

Which meant it wasn't going to be easy for her to dig herself out of that hole, especially since she couldn't rely on the sale of what little livestock she had left.

Ramon stood at the counter, trying to wrap his mind around Alana's dilemma. He glanced at the clock on the wall. It was nearly five o'clock. "Thanks, Ben. I appreciate your help."

As he stepped away from the counter, he stopped short and turned back to his father's old friend. "Would you do me a favor, Ben?"

"Sure thing."

"Call me if Hastings or his investigator comes around again, okay?"

"You got it. Tell your old man hello for me. It's been too damned long since we got together. It's time for another barbecue in his backyard. This time I'll supply the meat and the beer."

"I'll tell him."

Ramon walked out the door as if the news about the Texas rancher and his investigator didn't faze him. But it did. He found it all troubling. Something wasn't right.

Who the hell was Adam Hastings? Had he heard that the Lazy M had fallen on bad times? Was he trying to pick up the ranch at a fire sale? Why go to the trouble of investigating a property that wasn't even on the market?

Ramon had half a notion to call Callie and let her know what he'd just learned, but he decided to hold off until he knew more. She had enough on her plate these days, and he'd rather provide her with some peace of mind than give her cause to worry.

Damn. He had an odd yet growing need to protect Callie, a compulsion he'd never felt quite so intensely before. And it wasn't just sympathy causing it to flare up.

Like it or not, he cared more for her than he'd expected to. And he might even be falling for her.

He really should be glad that she'd stopped him from kissing her again back at the ranch. But for some damned reason, even though getting romantically involved with her could ruin a great friendship, he wasn't.

But if truth be told, kissing her wasn't the problem. His growing desire for her had begun to mess up their friendship already.

Ramon's first meeting with the political consultant had gone well, and he'd agreed to use the man's services—not just for the mayoral election, but for mapping out a run for the state senate in the not-too-distant future. So they'd started to meet regularly. As soon as they'd wrapped things up, he drove to Fairborn Medical Center to check on Katie.

He entered the lobby at a quarter past seven, took the elevator up to the second floor and walked to her room. The door was open, but instead of just walking in, he knocked once on the doorjamb.

"Katie?" he asked softly.

Her head turned, and when she spotted him, she managed a frail grin. "Hey, Coach."

He entered the room, where she lay in a hospital bed, her dark hair snarled and tangled, her face pale, an IV in her arm.

"How are you doing?" he asked.

"Okay, I guess." She squinted, then licked her lips. "It really hurts when the pain meds wear off."

"I'm sure it does." He eased closer to her bedside.

"How are the boys?"

"They're worried about you, but I told them you'd be back in fighting shape in no time. So they're doing okay. They seemed happy when I dropped them off at the ranch with Callie. If you don't mind, I'm going to take her up on her offer to help us out with them."

"That's okay. Thanks." Katie closed her eyes as the automatic blood pressure cuff began to pump.

Ramon checked the monitor, watching for the final numbers to pop up. Not that he was too sure what it all meant.

When the pressure in the cuff went down to normal, Katie's eyes opened and she looked at him, both pain and worry sketched across her face.

"If it makes you feel better," he said, "after I dropped Jesse and Mark off at Callie's, I hung around for a while. They had an afternoon snack. Cookies and milk. They were about to tackle their homework when I left. And believe it or not, there wasn't a single complaint."

At that she smiled, but her appreciation didn't last more than a couple of beats. The relief in her expression morphed into a grimace.

"Should I ask the nurse to give you something for pain?" he asked.

"No. That's okay. He came in before you got here. And he shot the medication into my IV. He said it would take a few minutes to kick in."

Ramon shoved his hands in his front pockets. He'd never been especially comfortable in a hospital setting, and he could use her discomfort as a reason to go. But he couldn't very well leave. Not until Katie felt better or drifted off to sleep.

"Coach," she said as her tired eyes met his. "I'm sorry."

"About what? Having appendicitis? That wasn't your fault. It couldn't be helped."

"I know, but I should've gone to Urgent Care when you suggested it. But I didn't. And now I have to stay a lot longer than I would have if I'd taken your advice."

"Maybe so, but how were you supposed to know it wasn't a stomach bug or something you ate?"

"I guess you're right…" She closed her eyes again, clearly in pain. "Tell Callie I really appreciate her keeping the boys for me. That's a big help. A huge one. But…"

A tear trickled down her cheek.

Damn. He wasn't keen on providing emotional

support, either. Jillian had been right about that.
But he couldn't very well skirt the issue now. Not
when Katie needed him.

He walked to the bed and took her hand in his.
"But what? You're worried about more than just
your brothers. What is it?"

She gave his hand a frail squeeze, then opened
her eyes. "I'm worried about school. And losing
my jobs—both of them."

From what he knew, she was taking two college
classes, and then there was her job cleaning bathrooms for the city, not to mention whatever she did
at the veterinary clinic. She'd be in the hospital for
at least a week, and then with the recovery time…?

"Let's take this step by step, Katie. I'll go to the
school on Monday and see if I can talk to your professors. Under the circumstances, I'm sure they'll
make allowances for your absence. I'm also going
to talk to your boss at the city and to the vet. I'm
sure they'll cut you some slack. And I'll help cover
the rent until you get back on your feet. It'll all
work out."

At that, she began to cry. "I don't know what to
say, Coach. You've been so good to us. Not just to
the boys, but to me, too. It might take a while, but
I promise to repay you."

"You don't have to. One day, when you become
a veterinarian, you'll run into someone who can't
afford the treatment for their pet. And you can

make up for my help then. That's what paying it forward means."

She sniffled. "I'm such a blubbering mess. This is embarrassing."

"You've been through a lot. You've been sick, had major surgery and now you're on pain meds and massive antibiotics. Don't blame yourself for not being at one hundred percent."

"Okay. You're right." She lifted the hand that wasn't tethered to the IV pole and swiped it under her eyes.

"And there's something else you should know. When you're released from the hospital, Callie and her friend Alana invited you to stay at the ranch while you recover. You and your brothers can go home once you're feeling up to it."

Tears welled in her eyes again. "That would be awesome, Coach. Will you please thank them for me?"

"Will do. And don't worry about finances. I'll help out until you're back on your feet."

"I can't let you do that…"

"Why not?"

She seemed to think on that awhile. Or maybe the pain meds had begun to kick in, because her eyes closed, and she didn't say another word.

He watched for a couple of minutes. Once he was sure the medication had kicked in and she'd dozed off, he left the room and headed down the hospital corridor to the elevator.

His thoughts drifted to Callie, as they seemed to do a lot these days. He had the urge to call her— just to hear her voice. But he tamped it down. Hell, they'd just talked a few hours ago.

Still, as he walked out the lobby doors and sucked in a breath of the crisp night air, he reached for his cell and called, anyway. There were a lot of reasons to touch base with her this evening. Hearing her voice had nothing to do with it. Right?

She answered without saying hello. "Hey, how's it going? Did you get a chance to see Katie?"

"Yes, I just left the hospital. She's in a lot of pain, but the meds seem to help. How're the boys doing?"

"They're fine, but we did have a little a mishap right before dinner."

Uh-oh. "What happened?"

"There's a dead tree on the side of the yard. We'd planned to have someone dig it up and haul it away, but we hadn't gotten around to it yet, which is too bad. It fell over this afternoon and smashed the chicken coop."

It hadn't rained lately, so the ground wasn't too wet. And it hadn't been the least bit windy. "The tree just toppled over?"

"I'm afraid it had a little help. The boys found a rope in the barn and decided to make a swing.

So the extra weight and a little motion was all it took to knock it down."

"Are the boys okay?"

"Yes, and feeling very apologetic. The hens are okay, too, but they really freaked out."

"There goes your egg production for a while."

Callie laughed. The soft lilt in her voice set off a warmth in his chest and drew a smile across his lips.

"We can get by without eggs for a while," she said. "Alana and I are just glad the boys and the hens weren't hurt."

"Were you able to patch up that coop?"

"No. We're going to have to do some serious repair work. So we brought the hens into the mud-room to spend the night."

Ramon rolled his eyes. "That'll be a bit messy."

"I'm sure it will be, but we didn't know what else to do. We don't want a wild animal to get to them. And the barn door has a few missing slats, which would make it too easy for them to escape."

Ramon couldn't help but laugh. "I'll stop by and see what I can do."

"Don't be silly, Ramon. It's already dark. And the chickens are safe for now."

She was right. And he hadn't eaten dinner yet. "I'll tell you what. I'll come by tomorrow, but it won't be first thing. My dad's out of town this week, and his foreman had a family wedding to attend in Idaho. So I'm doing the morning chores. Once I'm done, I'll come by the ranch and help you get those chickens back in their coop."

"Are you sure you don't mind?" she asked.

"Not at all." He'd stop by the feed store first to pick up some chicken wire, wood and nails. That ought to take care of repairing the coop. But he'd also have to deal with the tree. "Do you have a tractor?"

"There's one in the barn, but I don't know if it runs."

"Then I'll bring my toolbox."

She let out a soft sigh. "I hate to have you go out of your way."

"Why? You're going out of your way by helping with the boys. What kind of guy would I be if I couldn't help you out in some way in return?"

She paused for a couple of beats. "Okay, then. I'll see you tomorrow."

Looking forward to it, he thought. But he kept that to himself and ended the call instead.

Who would have guessed that hauling off a dead tree and fixing a broken-down chicken coop would sound like a nice way to spend the afternoon?

On Saturday morning, after breakfast, Callie let the chickens outside to free range. Then Alana and the boys helped her clean out the mudroom and mop the floor using a disinfectant.

What a mess that had been. Splashes of water, a dusting of chicken scratch, fluffy little feathers here and there, not to mention the poop! And Mark found an egg near the laundry basket.

No wonder Ramon had laughed about her bringing the hens into the house last night. Thank goodness they would be back in their coop this afternoon.

"If you boys will get washed up," Alana said, "I'll take you to visit your sister."

"Cool!" Mark said. "Come on, Jess. I'll race you to the bathroom."

Watching the brothers dash off, Callie chuckled and shook her head. They really were such sweet boys. Katie was doing a terrific job with them.

"Callie," Alana said, "I thought we'd take them to get hamburgers for lunch, and then we can catch a movie at the Reel Deal, the dollar theater next to the drugstore."

"That sounds like fun, and I'd like to go with you, but Ramon is stopping by sometime this afternoon to haul off that tree and repair the chicken coop. So I need to be here when he comes."

"Oh, that's so nice of him! Please thank him for me in case I don't get back in time. We don't want those hens to spend another night in the house. It's bad enough cleaning up after them outside."

"I couldn't agree more."

After Alana and the boys drove away, Callie

took a shower. Then she spent the morning organizing the pantry while doing the laundry, starting with the clothes she'd worn while cleaning up after the hens. She'd just switched a second load of clothing from the washer to the dryer when she heard the sound of an approaching vehicle.

A rush of excitement zipped through her, jump-starting her heart. That had to be Ramon.

She hurried to the front of the house and swung open the door. Dressed in a long-sleeved black T-shirt, worn jeans and scuffed boots, the dashing town council member looked more like a cowboy today. He held an army-green metal toolbox in one hand and balanced three large pizza boxes with the other.

A boyish grin lit his eyes. "I hope you haven't fixed lunch yet. But if you did, you can save this for dinner."

"Thank you." She stepped aside to let him enter the house. "That was sweet—and thoughtful. But I've already eaten. And on top of that, I'm the only one here. Alana took to boys to visit their sister and then to a movie."

As he entered the living room, she reached to take the three boxes. "This is going to be enough for several meals."

"It probably is. But I wasn't sure who liked what, so I figured I'd bring a variety. You guys can have your choice of cheese, pepperoni or veggie pizza."

"How's Katie doing?" she asked.

"I haven't talked to her since last night."

"Come with me," Callie said. "I'm going to take this to the kitchen."

Ramon followed her out of the room. "I don't think I mentioned it, but when I told Katie that you and Alana invited her to recover at the ranch, she was touched. And she cried."

"I'm glad we can take some of the worry off her mind." Callie moved things around in the refrigerator and made room for the pizza boxes.

"Do you mind if I head outside?" he asked. "I'd like to check out the tree and the coop to see what I'm up against."

"Not at all. I'll go with you."

She led him through the mudroom, with its lingering smell of soap and disinfectant, and out the back door to the coop, where the tree had smashed in the roof and knocked the wire door off the hinge.

"Alana tried to lift it," Callie said, "but it was too heavy for her. The boys wanted to help, but I wouldn't let them. We were afraid they'd get hurt."

"Good idea. Where's the tractor?"

She led him to the back of the barn, where a small tractor was parked, its once-yellow paint weathered by the elements. Hopefully, the engine was in better shape.

"It's a Caterpillar D-2." Ramon placed the toolbox on the ground, then studied the engine, moving a couple of wires, checking various parts. "It looks like it's got a pony motor. So it won't need a battery. These things are pretty reliable. We might need a spark plug and some clean fuel, but we'll probably be able to get it running again."

"You've worked on tractors before?"

He glanced up from the engine and tossed her a charming, good ol' boy grin. "I grew up on a ranch, remember?" Then he winked. "I have a lot of talents you aren't aware of."

She didn't doubt that for a moment. Heck, the ones she was aware of were pretty darned impressive. And when he bent to look over the engine again, he provided her with a striking view of his denim-clad butt, a red rag tucked into his back pocket. He might look like a cowboy, but he worked on that tractor like a competent mechanic.

Either way, for a town councilman with an MBA degree, Ramon was clearly at home on a ranch. He was good with kids, too. Not just Jesse and Mark, but his entire team. No matter what he might say, he really was a true family man.

A dreamy what-if floated through her mind, and hope rose like a red birthday balloon until reality provided a pinprick. Ramon deserved to create a family of his own, rather than taking on one that consisted of three stepchildren.

No, Callie, with all her baggage, was the last woman in the world he should get involved with, even if she'd like nothing more than to hang her heart on that man.

"Can you hand me a screwdriver?" he asked. "It's in my toolbox."

"Sure." She strode to the small green metal case he'd brought with him, glad she could be helpful.

After retrieving the tool, she handed it to him. Her fingers brushed his, sending a warm shiver through her veins, and she nearly lost her grip on the tool.

She had half a notion to retreat, to head back to the house before he realized how his very presence affected her. But she remained at his side, watching him work and savoring the scents of soap, musk and man.

"It's going to need a new fuel pump soon," he said. "But I think we can get by without it today."

"Good."

He straightened, turned to her and smiled. As his gaze locked on hers, his smiling expression drifted into serious waters. He reached up and brushed a strand of hair from her cheek.

"Oops. I got a little grease on you." He reached around his back, removed the rag he'd tucked into his pocket and dabbed it against her cheek.

Her lips parted at his gentle touch, and his movements stalled.

Her heart began to race. She knew where this was going and what would happen—if she let it.

Tell him no. Not here. Not now.

But this time, when he slipped his arms around her waist and drew her close, she shut out the voice of common sense. And when he lowered his mouth to hers, she didn't care about anything other than kissing him once more, even if it was for the very last time.

Chapter Eleven

Callie's lips parted, allowing Ramon's tongue to dip and twist and explore every nook and cranny of her sweet mouth until he didn't think he could get enough. The kiss intensified, heating his blood as it pumped through his veins, urgent and pounding out in need.

He might have grease on his hands, which would dirty her clothing or smudge her skin, but he was too caught up in her tantalizing taste, in her desperate embrace, to give it another thought.

Their breaths mingled, their tongues tangled and his heart raced. Kissing didn't get any better than this. His hands slid up and down her back, then along the slope of her hips. He gripped her derriere with both hands and pulled her flush against his erection.

He wanted her so badly that pure desire made his head spin, but making love would have to be her idea. He wouldn't push.

But damn. If she didn't put a stop to this kiss, they'd have to seek out a soft pile of straw, where they could lie down, stretch out and do what felt like the most natural thing in the world.

Finally, she drew her mouth from his and placed her hand on his chest, where his heart pounded like some savage beast. Her gaze locked on his, but he didn't dare say a word.

Please don't stop us, Callie. Not this time.

He studied her eyes, where a battle was clearly raging. Yet he had no doubt that she wanted to make love as much as he did.

"What are we going to do about this?" he asked.

For a couple of beats, while desire surged through him and hope soared, Callie remained silent, lost in the internal struggle. Then she reached for his hand and led him out of the barn, across the yard and into the house.

Ramon didn't say another word for fear he'd break the magical mood or cool the heat that had consumed them both. He'd had opportunities to have sex several times since his divorce, but he'd turned them down. And now he was glad he had.

Making love with Callie was going to be special, and it was worth the wait.

In silence, she led him into a bedroom—hers, he assumed—and shut the door. Once inside, he kissed her again—long and deep. He savored the feel of her in his arms, every soft curve, until it became clear that a kiss would no longer be enough.

He pulled his mouth from hers, but he didn't release her. Instead, he rested his forehead against the top of her head, breathing in the floral scent of her shampoo.

"I haven't had sex since my wife left," he admitted. "But I want you to know that this is more than just satisfying a physical need. I care about you."

"I know," she said. "I…care about you, too." She blessed him with a shy smile, then reached for the hem of her T-shirt, lifted it over her head and tossed it aside, revealing a satiny pink bra that barely contained her breasts.

He stood in stunned appreciation as she peeled off her yoga pants. Callie was a dream come true, his dream. And all he could think was, *Don't pinch me. I don't want to wake up.*

Once she stood before him wearing only that pretty pink bra and matching panties, he removed his shirt and pants. Her gaze never left his as he bared himself to her in a slow, deliberate fashion.

She skimmed her nails across his chest, heating his blood and sending a tingle shivering through

his veins. Then she reached behind her, slowly un-
hooked her bra and tossed it aside, releasing two
beautiful breasts, the dusky nipples begging to be
touched. Kissed. Tasted. Teased.

Even the bulge in her belly, where the babies
grew, intrigued him.

"You're beautiful, Callie. More so than I'd imagined." He reached for her breasts, kneading them
in his hands, caressing them. Then he knelt before her and took a nipple in his mouth, tonguing
it, sucking it.

When he straightened, she rose up on her tip-
toes and kissed him again, long and deep. Would
he ever get enough of her? It didn't seem likely.

When they both came up for air, he said, "I'm
not sure where we're going with this, Callie, but I
like the direction it's taking."

He waited for her to agree, and when she didn't,
he couldn't help prodding her to speak. "What do
you think?"

The question stunned her, drawing her out of
the sweet, heated moment. Giving him an answer
meant facing reality.

"I'm not sure what to think," she said, her voice
as soft and wistful as the happily-ever-after dream
that always seemed to elude her.

The idea of newborn twins hadn't seemed to
give him much pause, but how would he feel about
adding a college student to the mix, a kid who'd

always been more of an adult than a child, but who still needed his mother?

She'd definitely have to tell Ramon she had a son. But not here, not before making love.

Realizing they might never have this chance again, she convinced herself that they'd gone too far to stop now. She'd just have to deal with regrets later.

She reached up, cupped his jaw and drew his mouth back to hers.

They continued to kiss, to taste, to stroke and explore each other until they were both drowning in desire.

She drew back long enough to climb on the bed and settle on top of the floral comforter. Then she opened her arms, silently asking him to join her.

When he did, they kissed again, their bodies bare, their skin slick, until it was hard to catch a breath, until she was wet and ready and aching with need.

As he hovered over her, she gazed into his passion-filled eyes. He entered her slowly at first, but as her body responded to his, as she arched up to meet each of his thrusts, in and out, the room stood still. Life stood still. Only they moved; only they mattered.

They came together in a sexual explosion that nearly stole her breath away. But it didn't matter. She didn't dare breathe anyway, didn't dare do anything to end the sweet moment.

As they lay in the ebb and flow of their release, she held him close, savoring his musky scent and basking in the stunning afterglow of the best sex she'd ever had. Not that she was all that experienced. But still…

He pressed a kiss on her brow. "That was amazing."

"I know." She snuggled close to him and rested her head against his shoulder, taking what he had to offer for as long as she could, knowing it wouldn't last. There'd be no golden rings to snag on this merry-go-round. Their sweet ride wasn't going anywhere but in a circle. And it would come to an end before the semester ended.

Even if her cerebral son didn't fault her for getting involved so soon after her breakup with Garrett, how would he feel about having a man in his life, someone who didn't have any of the same interests he had, like science and math and reading the *Journal of the Medical Association*?

Summer break was just around the corner. And she'd have to address the fact that she hadn't been honest—with either Ramon or Micah.

She had no idea how Ramon would react when he learned she had a teenage son. But a more pressing and worrisome question came to mind.

Callie adored Micah and had always been proud of him.

So why had she kept him a secret?

* * *

After making love with Ramon on Saturday, Callie had remained quiet and pensive, troubled over how and when to reveal her secret. She'd even kept her thoughts to herself after Ramon had gone outside to finish the work he'd started before lust had sidetracked them.

He'd used the tractor to remove the tree from the coop, then he'd worked on getting the wire roofing repaired and the gate fixed. She'd stood by his side, ready to help however needed, but their conversation was limited to small talk.

Fortunately, Alana brought the boys home from their visit with their sister, which lightened the mood with happy chatter.

Ramon stayed to eat warmed-up pizza with them for dinner, and if he'd sensed that something was off, he didn't say. When the evening ended, Callie had walked him to the door, and he'd given her a sweet, almost chaste kiss goodbye.

"I'll call you tomorrow," he'd said.

And he did. She'd tried to keep her tone upbeat during the call, but on the inside she was one hot mess.

"I'm not sure when I can pick up the boys," he'd said. "Sarge, my dad's prize bull, tore through the barbed-wire fence and ran off. I managed to catch the ornery brute, but he got caught in the wires and cut himself up. I've got a call in to the vet.

And to top it off, it's going to take some time to repair the fence."

"Don't worry about the boys," she told him. "I'll keep them another night and get them to school tomorrow."

"Thanks, Callie. What would I do without you?"

He'd be fine. But she couldn't help wondering what she was going to do without him.

On Monday morning, after dropping the boys off at school, Callie hurried to the Meadowlark Café.

"Thanks for opening for me," Callie told Shannon. "I know you're not an early bird by nature, so I really appreciate it."

"No problem. You've covered my butt quite a few times. If you hadn't, Gloria would have fired me a long time ago." Shannon glanced at the clock that hung behind the register. "But I'd better jam if I'm going to make it to my English class on time. It's a long walk."

"Would you like to borrow my car?" Callie asked.

"That's cool of you to offer, but I don't have a driver's license. Gloria refused to sign for me when I was sixteen. I should probably check into getting one now that I'm of age, but what's the use? I don't have wheels, anyway."

Shannon had no more than grabbed her backpack from behind the counter, when Marissa Garcia walked in. The attractive brunette in her midtwenties worked as a bookkeeper, although

Callie wasn't sure where. She was an attractive young woman with big green eyes and long, wavy hair.

"Good morning," Callie said. "Take any seat you'd like."

"Actually, I'm not here to have breakfast. I'd like to talk to the owner."

"Her name is Jasmine Daniels," Callie said. "She usually comes in around four in the afternoon."

"The company I worked for downsized," Marissa said, "so I'm out of a job."

Callie could connect the dots. If the woman was looking for office work, she was probably out of luck, but it wasn't her place to say so. "Jasmine handles the bookwork herself, but who knows? She might be interested in hiring someone to help out."

"I haven't been able to pick up anything full-time, so I've lined up a few consulting jobs. I'm good when it comes to looking at the books and finding ways to cut corners or increase production. I'm already doing some work for Darla's Doughnuts and at The Mane Event, the new salon down the street. I was hoping I could do the same for the Meadowlark Café."

She might be able to give Jasmine some ideas on increasing business. But what about the ranch? Alana and Callie could use all the help they could get. And neither of them believed Alana's attendance at that cattle symposium had been a worthwhile investment—other than Alana getting laid by a handsome guy she'd never see again.

"You know," Callie said, "I'm not sure what you charge, or if we can afford it, but my friend needs someone to help her come up with a budget and a marketing plan at her ranch."

"I won't kid you. I'm a little desperate right now, and I haven't built up a client base, so I'm willing to work out a deal. I can drive out tomorrow if that would work for you."

"I have Wednesday off," Callie said. "And I'd like to hear what you have to say. Can we make it Wednesday morning?"

"Of course." Marissa flashed a smile. "Thanks for the opportunity to prove myself."

Before Callie could respond, the door squeaked open and Ramon walked in. Her breath caught, and her heart slipped into overdrive.

He shot a glance at Marissa, who flushed a pretty shade of pink when he offered her a dazzling smile. "Hey. How's it going?"

"I'm not ready to throw in the towel yet," Marissa said. "You were right, though. Things seem to be working themselves out."

The two knew each other? Had they talked about Marissa's employment—or the lack of it?

Callie's gut clenched, and a green-eyed twinge of jealousy struck. If truth be told, Marissa would

be a lot better match for Ramon than she'd ever
be—and not just because of the age difference.

"Well," Marissa said, "I'd better go. I have a
couple of other businesses to visit this morning."

"I'll talk to you later," he said.

Oh yeah? When was later?

Callie had never suffered from jealousy, and
she sure as heck didn't like feeling that way now.
Even though she knew how this thing with Ramon
was bound to end, she didn't like thinking of any
other woman making love with him.

As Marissa walked out of the café, Ramon
turned his attention to Callie. "How'd the boys
do last night?"

"Great." Unable to quell her mounting curiosity, Callie said, "I see you and Marissa have met."

He nodded. "Sometimes I stop by Darla's and
pick up a box of doughnuts as a treat for the staff
at city hall."

That made sense, she supposed. "How's Sarge?"

"The vet says he should be fine. It was nothing
a few stitches and an antibiotic won't fix."

Callie glanced at the clock, then back to Ramon.
"You're coming in later than usual. Did you have
an early-morning meeting?"

"I had breakfast with the Rotary Club, but I
wouldn't mind getting a coffee to go."

"You got it." Glad to have a reason to focus on
something other than the man who'd swept her

off her feet on Saturday afternoon and turned her life on end, she headed for the coffeepot, filled a to-go cup with the fresh brew and then returned to where he stood near the door. "Here you go. It's on the house."

"You sure?"

Callie wasn't sure about anything when he was around, but she said, "Of course. Jasmine likes us to keep the regulars happy so they'll keep coming back."

"Do you get off at four?" he asked.

"That's the plan. Shannon is supposed to take the afternoon/evening shift. Hopefully, she'll get here on time. She's been a little more dependable lately."

"I get the feeling she doesn't arrive on time just to upset her aunt Gloria," Ramon said.

Callie smiled. "I've thought the same thing. It seems like a passive-aggressive way to set Gloria off. Shannon can also be a little ditzy at times. But not in a bad way. She's actually very sweet and likable."

Ramon nodded in agreement. "I called a practice today and thought I'd pick up the boys from school. When it's over, I'll take them to the ranch and pick up some groceries on the way."

"You don't have to do that," she said. "We still have plenty left from your last shopping trip. I hope you'll stay for dinner."

He tossed her a wink that darn near turned her inside out. "I hoped you'd say that."

Callie glanced around the café. Several patrons sat at the counter, and a foursome ate a hearty breakfast in the corner booth. But no one was in the near vicinity. Still, she lowered her voice. "About Saturday. Let's take things slow, okay? Just one day at a time."

"How about one night at a time?"

Bedtime thoughts swirled in her mind, just as they must be doing in his. He probably imagined the two of them curled up in bed, enjoying the afterglow of another amazing lovemaking session.

Callie could imagine that, too, but at the same time, she heard the cries of fussing babies wanting to be fed, as well as a ringing cell phone, with Micah calling for a little maternal reassurance because some dumb jock embarrassed him again—all in the name of frat boy fun.

No, she had to come clean and tell Ramon that things weren't what they seemed, no matter the cost.

But before she could ponder the right words to say, he asked, "How about going out with me Saturday night? I thought we could go into Kalispell for dinner and a movie. And, if you'd like and Alana doesn't mind keeping the boys, we can also have breakfast on Sunday morning."

Apparently, he had no idea what taking it slow meant. But she couldn't skirt the issue any longer.

"I can't do that," she said, her voice whisper

soft. "Not until I tell you something I should have mentioned a long time ago."

His smile didn't falter. "What's that?"

She took a deep breath, pushed through her reluctance. "I have a son."

Callie had a son?

Ramon hadn't seen that coming. And apparently the kid was old enough not to live with her.

"His name is Micah," she said. "And he's coming home for a visit."

Clearly there was a lot he didn't know. "Where does Micah go to school?" he asked.

"In Texas. He's a freshman at Baylor University."

Her son was a college student? He'd known she was probably older than he was, and that hadn't really bothered him. But how old *was* she? He wouldn't ask, but he could do the math. She may not look it, but with a kid in college, she had to be…pushing forty. And that meant Ramon was closer in age to her son than he was to Callie.

"I…don't know what to say."

Callie stiffened, clearly not happy with his lame response. And he couldn't blame her. But for the life of him, he hadn't been able to come up with anything else to say, other than she'd been right: there were a lot of reasons a long-term relationship between the two of them wouldn't last. But hadn't they already dived headfirst into something?

Ramon continued to study her, to ponder the news she'd just given him. He still cared about her. And he definitely wanted to make love with her again. But he had a lot to think about, a lot to consider. And he'd be damned if he'd do or say something without considering the repercussions.

"Are you upset that I didn't tell you sooner?" she asked, her voice whisper soft. "Before we made love?"

He should be, he supposed. "I'm not exactly upset. Not really." He just needed time to sort it all out. Hell, he was only twenty-eight years old—and embarking on a political career. Everything would be fodder for the media. "We can talk more about this tonight. Okay?"

She nodded, and he left the café with his to-go cup of coffee. But he no longer felt like drinking it. He was too busy trying to wrap his brain around Callie's unexpected news.

It's not like he wanted to cut bait and run. But her revelation brought up an issue he'd tried to forget.

Jillian had claimed he wasn't mature enough to be a parent, that he wouldn't be "emotionally available" to a child. He'd thought her accusation was baseless. But had she been right?

Ramon's mother had bailed on him when he'd been six. He could remember the day his father had told him she'd left for good.

But I don't understand, Daddy. Where did she go? Why isn't she coming back?

Don't you worry, his father had said. *You and I are going to be fine without her, son. In fact, we're better off now that she's gone. Just wait and see.*

Nearly two years later, they got word that the man she'd run off with had died in a barroom brawl. By then, Ramon and his father had pulled together and were doing okay without her. He hadn't expected her to return to Fairborn, but he hadn't understood why she'd never even tried to contact him. And it stayed with him his entire life.

Jillian had claimed he had relationship issues. He'd talked to his therapist about the possibility that he might have fears of abandonment, but she hadn't thought that was the case. Besides, Callie was nothing like his mother. She had a sweet, maternal side to her—and it turned out she already had a son, with two more kids on the way. Ramon found her more than a little special.

In his heart, he didn't think his mother's abandonment had anything to do with his feelings for Callie now. Or how he'd felt about the news that she had a grown son. But would the age difference be a problem in the future?

He'd like to believe that it wouldn't.

Either way, they were in pretty deep already. They'd made love. Was it too late for them to go back to being just friends?

And if so, would that be enough for him?

Chapter Twelve

Over the next couple of days, Callie and Ramon had spoken very little to each other. At least, not about the afternoon they'd made love or what that might mean for them in the future. Their only conversations, as friendly as they'd been, had taken place on the days she dropped Mark and Jesse off at practice or whenever he brought them to the ranch to spend the night.

He'd been kind when he'd arrived with the boys in tow, and he usually brought a bag of groceries or a gallon of milk with him, but unlike he'd done in the past, he didn't accept a dinner invitation. Callie really wasn't surprised, though. She'd known all along that she'd brought too much baggage to the game. It was just that, for once in her life, she wished she'd been wrong.

On top of that, he hadn't stopped by the Meadowlark Café to eat, either, although he had mentioned that he'd been incredibly busy. From his tone and his facial expressions, Callie had no reason to be skeptical of his claim, although she still couldn't shake the feeling that he was avoiding her. And if that was the case, she really couldn't blame him. But she still felt a keen loss, and it hurt like hell.

On Wednesday morning, after taking the boys to school, Callie returned to the ranch to meet with Marissa. They'd agreed upon a reasonable fee for the consultation, but they only had to pay her if they felt her suggestions were helpful.

Callie had talked it over with Alana first and asked, "What do you think?"

"Why not? I blew money on that cattle symposium I attended, and it wasn't very helpful, especially when I hardly know which end of the cow I'm supposed to feed."

They'd both laughed at the joke that wasn't too far from the truth.

Now, as they stood on the front porch, waiting for Marissa to arrive, Alana asked, "Does she know we're struggling to make ends meet?"

"I didn't see any reason to pretend otherwise,"

Callie said. "I told her we're barely keeping afloat, and that we could use someone who had some financial expertise. There's got to be something we can do to make sure the ranch can turn a profit."

"Does she have any experience with cattle or ranching?"

Callie sucked in a deep breath and slowly blew it out. "No, I don't think so."

Alana cut a sideways glance and gave Callie the look. The kind a nanny shot a kid who'd told a big whopper. "I love you, Cal. And I appreciate how you jumped on Team Alana the minute I called you. But I'm not sure how this consultation is going to help."

"What do we have to lose?"

"Whatever Marissa ends up billing us."

They remained on the porch, waiting in silence, both lost in their thoughts, it seemed. Callie reached into her back pocket and pulled out her cell phone.

"Are you going to call her?" Alana asked.

"No, she'll be here. I just want to check my texts." Callie had gotten so caught up with the Johnson family, plus work and Ramon, that she hadn't been stressing over her son, which was probably a good thing. In the past, Alana had called her a helicopter mom. So by getting involved in her own everyday life, she might have unconsciously given Micah the space he needed to grow up and create a life of his own.

But that didn't mean she wasn't concerned. "Micah's due to arrive next week. And I haven't heard from him in days."

"I'd say that's a good thing. I realize he's only sixteen, but he's more adult than some of the men I've dated in the past. You need to cut him more slack, Cal."

Maybe so. And he was probably studying for finals, which were coming up soon. She closed the phone and slid it into her pocket, determined to call him this evening.

An engine sounded, and they both looked toward the driveway and watched a maroon-colored sedan, its paint faded, pull into the yard.

"Is that her?" Alana asked.

"Yes, it is."

Alana didn't have to say it. Callie knew what she was thinking. Marissa's car didn't look like one a successful accountant or consultant would drive. But what the heck. Alana and Callie weren't actually ranchers. Not by any stretch of the word.

The dogs, Rascal and Chewie, trotted up to the car, barking, but their tails were wagging. Marissa got out of her car and offered up a warm smile. "It was a little difficult to find, but I'm here."

"Thanks for coming." Callie stepped off the

porch with Alana on her heels and made her way toward Marissa, who'd stopped to pet the dogs.

Marissa straightened and scanned the grounds, taking in the house and the barn. "Nice place you have here."

"It has a lot of promise," Alana said. "But we're doing the best we can with what we've got to work with."

Marissa reached out and shook Alana's hand. "Thanks for giving me a chance to help you. Why don't we start by looking over the books?"

Alana led her to the small office inside the house, where Marissa got busy looking at ledgers, as well as the accounts payable and receivable.

Marissa asked quite a few questions, which Alana answered when she could. An hour later, she asked to go outside, where she looked over the inside of the barn, checked out the newly repaired chicken coop and even studied the small, scraggly, six-tree orchard from a distance.

"My first suggestion," Marissa said, as they returned to the front yard, where she'd parked her worn-out car, "is that you hold off on buying any cattle until you have the money to invest."

Alana shot a glance at Callie, one that said, *Thanks, Captain Obvious.*

Alana had a little left in the savings account she'd inherited from her grandfather, but she'd been using that for food and utilities, not to mention paying a little something toward the back taxes.

Callie had some cash stashed aside, too. But if she'd felt secure enough to tap into it, she would have purchased the Meadowlark Café from Jasmine. But the twins had given her a new priority. She placed her hand on her growing baby bump and caressed it. "So what do you suggest we do in the meantime, Marissa?"

"Have you considered planting a garden?"

"Yes," Alana said. "That's at the top of my to-do list. Growing our own vegetables will help offset our grocery bill."

"I'm not talking about food for your table. I'd like to see you plant a big garden, with a lot of variety. If you grew an abundance of squash, tomatoes, green beans and that sort of thing, you could sell produce at the farmers market in town."

Alana's eyes widened. "Oh my gosh. That's a great idea. I hadn't thought about that."

"While you're waiting to harvest your crops, you can buy more chickens. That way you can sell farm-fresh eggs, too." Marissa turned and pointed to the orchard. "Are those cherry trees?"

"Yes," Callie said. "They need pruning, but they're producing fruit."

"That's good." Marissa placed her hands on her denim-clad hips and smiled. "Do either of you know how to bake?"

"I do," Alana said, "especially cookies. I have a ton of recipes."

"I can see where you're going with this," Callie said. "We can sell home-baked items, too. I'm not a whiz in the kitchen, but I'll start watching the food channel on TV. And you'd be surprised at what you can learn on YouTube."

"How about jams and jellies?" Alana added. "We'll need to do something with those cherries."

"Bingo!" Marissa broke into a happy grin. "That ought to help you build up the coffers."

It would. But they'd still have to invest in canning jars, baking tins, not to mention flour, sugar, etc. But now that they had an actual game plan, Callie wouldn't mind drawing from her savings for the up-front money.

"You should probably consider giving the buyers a discount if they bring back their empty jars," Marissa said. "That way, you won't have to constantly purchase new ones."

"Wow," Alana said. "I was really beginning to lose hope, but now I'm excited. How much do we owe you?"

"How about fifty dollars?" Marissa asked.

"Done." Alana reached out and shook her hand again. "I'll cut you a check now, and once we start selling our wares at the farmers market, we'll give you the family discount."

For the first time since moving to the Lazy M,

Callie had a solid reason to believe that she and Alana would be able to turn things around, and that the run-down Rancho Esperanza would become a producing ranch—just in a different way than they'd ever imagined. All they needed to do now was to get those back taxes paid.

Alana hadn't told Callie how far behind Jack McGee had gotten—or how much she'd paid toward the delinquency so far. But surely it couldn't be that much.

Everything was finally coming together, and the future looked bright. Well, at least, as far as Rancho Esperanza was concerned.

Callie couldn't claim the same bright outlook for herself. Sure, Micah would be coming home to visit. And the doctor had assured her the babies were both healthy and growing.

But when it came to her and Ramon, everything was falling apart.

Ramon had promised Katie that he would pick her up from the hospital once she was discharged, so when she called him with the news that the doctor was signing the paperwork to let her go home, he had to reschedule a couple of meetings—but he was there, as promised.

After leaving the hospital, he drove Katie to the apartment to pick up a few personal items she might need for her stay on the ranch. He had some things to tell her, but he'd held off until she was well on the mend. And this seemed like the right time.

"The good news," he said, "is that your professors are willing to work with you so you won't have to file an incomplete or take those classes during summer school."

"Oh, thank goodness. I've been trying to keep up with the reading, but I had two papers to write, and I couldn't do it at the hospital. I'm also taking calculus this term, so I'm going to have a lot of catching up to do." She blew out a sigh, then glanced across the console, no doubt coming to grips with what he hadn't yet told her. "So what's the bad news?"

Damn. He hated to break it to her, but there was no way to soften the blow. "You're going to have to look for a new job. Dr. Rockland said you're great with the animals, and he didn't want to lose you, but he had to find a replacement. He needed the help immediately."

"I had a feeling he was going to say that."

"On the bright side, he told me he'd be happy to rehire you in the future—or write a letter of recommendation."

She blew out a ragged sigh and rested her head against the passenger window. "I don't blame him. He counts on an assistant to feed and care for the animals. It's just that I loved that job."

Neither of them spoke for the rest of the drive—Katie because she was probably lost in thought, and Ramon because he was afraid he'd say the wrong thing and didn't want to make her feel any worse.

When they finally pulled into the yard, Jesse and Mark, who'd been sitting on the porch—no doubt waiting for them to arrive—jumped up and ran toward the vehicle with the two ranch dogs on their heels.

They hurried to the passenger side, and as Katie climbed out, she held up her hand like a traffic cop. "Whoa, guys. Don't rush me. I'm still a little sore. I need gentle hugs."

Ramon stood back and watched the family reunion. The boys had visited Katie nearly every day while she'd been in the hospital, but they were clearly happy to have her "home," even if it was just a temporary stay until they could return to their apartment.

"First you gotta meet the dogs," Jesse told his big sister, "then me and Mark will show you all around the ranch. You're gonna love it here."

Ramon glanced at the house. He assumed he'd find Callie inside. He hadn't had a chance to talk to her, other than making small talk about the kids. So he owed her an adult conversation, even if he wasn't quite sure what to say.

The door squeaked open, and Callie stepped

onto the porch wearing a blue-and-yellow sundress and sandals. She'd never looked prettier.

She lifted her hand to shade the sun from her eyes and scanned the yard. "Where's Katie?"

"She's getting a tour of the ranch."

Callie tucked a long strand of golden-brown hair behind her ear.

"Do you have time to take a walk?" he asked.

"I guess so. I wanted to welcome Katie and show her the living quarters where she and the boys will stay, but I suppose that can wait."

Once she'd joined him in the yard, he placed his hand on the small of her back, guiding her toward the orchard. "I'm sorry I haven't had much time for you. I've been swamped all week. So I'd like to take you out to dinner tonight."

"Why? You don't owe me anything."

"Yes, I do. I've practically gone AWOL. And on top of that, we never really got the chance to talk about last Saturday afternoon—and how we each feel about it."

"I know better than to expect any more than… Well, more than once. At least I'll be left with a nice memory."

"I'll admit, when you mentioned your college-age son, it took me by surprise. But I'd still like to see you."

She slowed to a stop and turned to face him, her eyes narrowed, her cheeks flushed. "Listen,

I'm not as old as you might think I am, but I'm certainly old enough to know better. And making love with you wasn't a good idea. It's not like I'm in my early twenties with nothing to tie me down except a job."

At first, the age difference concerned him, but the longer he went without seeing her, the more he'd missed her, and it hadn't taken him very long to come to the conclusion that it really didn't matter to him. "I care about you, Callie. And while I'm not sure about the future or where we should go from here, it's crossed my mind that I might…" He paused, unsure of how to voice what he'd been pondering off and on for nearly a week.

Callie picked up the slack. "You don't have to say it. I already know. Our situation is complicated. *I'm* complicated. I have one kid and will soon have two more."

"I wouldn't consider a college student a kid," Ramon said. "Not that he won't be a part of your life, but he's not a minor."

"That's where you're wrong." She crossed her arms, and as she zeroed in on him, anger simmered in her eyes. "Micah is only sixteen."

At that, Ramon took a step back. "And he's in college? At Baylor?"

"Believe it or not, he's a premed student and has been taking an exceptionally heavy load each semester."

Ramon let out a long, slow whistle. "That's a huge accomplishment. Micah must be a genius."

"Yes, he's brilliant, but in many ways, he's still a kid. I didn't want him to move out of the house so young, but I couldn't very well hold him back."

Ramon could certainly understand that. Damn. He wasn't sure what to say, what to think. But an apology was probably in order. "I'm sorry, Callie."

"I'm sorry, too."

About what? Not telling him she had a son sooner? But if she had, would it have mattered? He wasn't sure.

There was so much he didn't know about her. So much she hadn't told him.

Stuff he might have asked. Unable to help himself, one question came to mind, an important one, and it rolled off the tip of his tongue. "What about his father?"

"He died. In motorcycle accident. He was only seventeen."

"And you raised Micah by yourself?"

"Pretty much. I was seventeen and I lived with my aunt at the time. She helped some, but mostly by providing a roof over our heads and food on the table."

"That must have been tough," he said. "I mean, having a baby when you were really only a kid yourself."

"It wasn't easy, but Micah made it all worth it."

He could understand that. He didn't respond immediately. Instead, he thought about all she'd had to deal with as a single mom. "You also must have grieved for Micah's father."

"His name was Derek. And yes, it hurt to lose him." She tucked a strand of hair behind her ear. "I loved him as much as a naive teenager could. He was brilliant."

"Like Micah."

"Yes, but—thankfully—Micah didn't inherit his wild side."

"Is that what attracted you to him?" Ramon asked.

She smiled wistfully. "I suppose so. He was, in many ways, my opposite. But mostly, I just wanted to be loved."

As footsteps sounded, she glanced over her shoulder. "There's Katie now. It looks like the tour is over. I really should talk to her. Do you mind if we discuss this later?"

"At dinner?" he asked.

"I don't know about that. You aren't the only one who's had concerns about us dating or…whatever. So there really isn't anything to talk about."

As she started toward Katie and the boys, Ramon fell into step beside her. "If you don't want to take the time to talk now or later tonight, that's fine. But we need to do it soon."

She nodded, but she continued to walk—probably trying to avoid him and this conversation.

"Callie," he said, taking her arm and pulling her to a stop before she got within hearing range of the others. "I don't think our friendship is going to take a hit because we made love. On the other hand, not having a heart-to-heart is bound to have an effect."

She studied him for a moment, nodded her agreement then strode toward Katie and the boys, leaving Ramon dumbfounded and a little unbalanced. But however he felt, he knew one thing: he wasn't going to be yet another jerk in Callie's life.

Eager to put an end to their conversation, Callie headed toward Katie and the boys.

Ramon had been right, though. They did need to talk, she supposed. But the thought of having that little heart-to-heart left her more unsettled than ever. She'd never liked sharing the painful things in her life, and losing Micah's father had only been one of them. As it was, she'd wanted nothing more than to leave the past behind.

As she approached the boys and their sister, she overheard Jesse talking to Katie. "You're going to love staying here. It's so fun. And the best part is the dogs."

"Don't forget having a great big yard," Mark added.

"The ranch is really cool," Katie said, before

turning her attention to Callie. "I know I'll like staying here. And if my incision didn't still hurt and I could move a little faster, being here would be a vacation."

"It's a peaceful setting," Callie said. "So I know exactly what you mean."

"My sister loves animals more than anything," Jesse said.

Katie ruffled the boy's hair. "Not more than you guys."

"But almost," Mark added. "That's why she wants to be a vet. And that's why she works at the dog hospital in town."

Katie's smile faded, and she blew out a sigh. "I'm not going to be working there anymore, but when I did, we took care of more than just dogs."

"Why'd you quit?" Jesse asked.

"After I got sick, they had to let me go."

Mark cut a sideways glance at Katie. "You lost your job?"

"Just one of them." Katie glanced at Ramon, who'd just joined them. "I'll find another one. Don't worry, I have money saved for this month's rent."

Been there, done that, Callie thought. Not that she and Alana had to worry about rent or a mortgage, but there were still property taxes, utility bills, groceries...

At that point, Alana joined them in the yard.

After greeting Katie, she said, "Boys, why don't you take your sister to the outbuilding we fixed up for you guys. She's had a long morning already, and I'm sure she'd like to get settled."

"Good idea," Katie said. "I'd better lie down for a while."

As the kids headed toward the outbuilding Jack had intended to offer to a ranch foreman, going so far as to re-roof it when the house and barn were in worse shape, Alana lifted her hand to shield her eyes from the sun. "Hastings called again. Can you believe it, Cal? That guy doesn't quit."

"Hastings?" Ramon asked. "What'd he want?"

"You know him?" Callie asked.

"I'm sorry for butting in. But no, I don't actually know him. It's just that he's gaining a reputation in these parts."

"I don't know what you heard about him, but he's determined to buy the ranch, even though I keep telling him it's not for sale." Alana swept her arm toward the pasture and the barn. "I mean, look at this place. I know it needs a lot of work, but it's home to me. And I'm not going to let it go, even though he's offered to pay me more than it's worth."

"That's odd," Ramon said.

Callie thought so, too.

"And this isn't the only ranch in the area he's trying to buy," Alana added.

"That seems a little fishy," Ramon said. "And as a town councilman, I want to know what he's up to."

Callie's arched a brow. "You don't suppose he suspects there's gold or oil or something of huge value in the area, do you?"

"I don't know what to think. But I'll let you know when I get some answers."

"Thanks," Alana said. "I'd really appreciate that. In the meantime, come on in the house. It's past noon, and lunch is ready."

"That sounds good," Ramon said. "I didn't have much in the way of breakfast."

As they headed toward the steps that led to the back door, Callie couldn't shake a dark, unsettling feeling. And not just because her friendship with Ramon would never be the same again. That was bad enough. But the peace she'd felt on Rancho Esperanza had begun to fade, and so had the hope they'd all clung to. Sure, Alana could sell the ranch and pocket a tidy sum. She could also purchase another property, one that didn't need as much work.

But Rancho Esperanza wasn't just a ranch. It was a family home, something Alana had never had before. If she sold—or God forbid, lost—the property, where would she be?

Where would they all be? Callie wondered. Because she'd begun to think of Rancho Esperanza as *her* home, too.

Chapter Thirteen

Ramon and the boys washed up in the mudroom while Alana put lunch on the table. Callie didn't seem to be happy he'd accepted Alana's invitation to join them, but he figured retreating now would only make things worse.

The hearty aroma of bacon had wafted in from the kitchen, which struck him as a breakfast smell rather than lunch. But it didn't matter. He was hungry.

"You guys can take whatever seat you want," Callie said. "I'll tell Katie lunch is ready and ask if she'd like to come to the table. She's had a big day, so it might be better if I take her meal to her."

After drying his hands, Ramon took a seat across from the boys.

Alana set a platter of BLTs on the table, next to a plate of sliced apples and a bowl of potato chips. "I know it's not much, but it's filling."

"You won't hear me complain," Ramon said. "This is the best meal I've had all day—and most of the week."

Ramon wasn't just being polite. He'd been eating at home the past few days until he could figure out what to do about his growing attraction to Callie, and he wasn't much of a cook.

He'd told her that he'd been busy, which was true. He'd been trying to pull together plans for a new community center in town, despite the financial issues, and he'd had meetings up the wazoo. His political agenda seemed to be coming together, but he couldn't say the same about his personal aspirations. He just couldn't seem to wrap his head around the thought of dating the mother of a teenager.

Dating? Who was he kidding? With Callie, he wanted much more, and the pros and cons had been ping-ponging through his mind all week. While the political ramifications were always significant—and he really did think he had the opportunity to help transform his hometown— to his surprise it was the personal reasons taking center stage.

For one, what kind of stepfather would he make to a boy genius? If Micah were a student athlete, they might have more in common. And brilliant Micah probably wasn't a typical teenager. Who knew how he'd feel about having a man in his mother's life? Resentful? Protective?

Yet once he'd returned to the ranch and saw her again today, the ping-pong game ceased. All he knew was how much he'd missed her.

Before he could take a bite of his sandwich, Callie and Katie joined them for lunch. Callie took a seat next to him, but Katie remained standing, her hand resting on the back of her chair as she looked first at Alana, then at Callie. "Thanks again for letting us stay with you. I don't know how I'll ever be able to repay you guys, but somehow, I will."

"You don't owe us anything," Callie said, her smile warm, her words sincere. "We both love children. And the house was too quiet before Jesse and Mark came to visit. It's been fun having them here. We're also looking forward to getting to know you better."

What a warm, amazing woman. Ramon had missed more than just looking into Callie's pretty blue eyes and seeing her smile. She had a generous spirit and a thoughtfulness he rarely saw in people.

"Mark and Jesse have been teaching me how to play catch," Callie said. "And we've watched a couple of cool movies in the evening after homework is done."

"Don't forget the popcorn she makes us," Jesse

chimed in. "And the root beer floats. You gotta try one, Katie. They're super good."

So what if Callie was five or six years older than Ramon? Age didn't matter when he liked every single thing about her, from her maternal side to her smile. And the feelings he was having for her ran a hell of a lot deeper than admiration.

"You know," Alana said, "I never really had a family when I grew up. So when I worked as a nanny, I enjoyed spending time with the kids, making cookies, playing games and that sort of thing. And as much as I love ranch life, I miss having children around. So thank you for being here—all three of you—and making Rancho Esperanza feel like a real home."

"Gosh, you make it sound like us being here is doing you a favor," Katie said.

Callie tossed a smile at the young woman. "In a way, you really are."

From what Ramon had gathered, Callie had never had a traditional family, either. Something the two friends had in common.

Maybe that's what drew him and Callie to Katie, Mark and Jesse. They were untraditional, too. But somehow, the trio had provided both Callie and Ramon with an idea of what a real family was supposed to be like.

Or maybe he was trying too hard to figure it all

out. Maybe there were some things best left alone. And some that were just meant to be enjoyed.

Only one question remained, and it was the most important of all: Did he enjoy it enough to make Callie a permanent part of his life?

He didn't know.

After lunch, Katie pushed back her chair and grimaced as she slowly got to her feet. "I think I'd better rest for a while."

"Good idea," Alana said.

"Can me and Jesse go out and play after we help with the dishes?" Mark asked.

"Don't worry about helping out this time," Alana told him. "There's hardly anything to wash up. So go on outside."

"I need to get back to town," Ramon said. "Will you walk me outside, Callie?"

She hesitated a moment, then she nodded and got up from the table.

"Thanks for lunch," he told Alana before heading toward the back door.

"You're welcome to join us anytime, Ramon."

As he and Callie stepped outside, he said, "The boys have a game on Saturday morning."

"I know. We have the schedule posted on the fridge. I can drop them off at the ball field around ten, but I can't stay and watch them play."

"Are you working?"

"No. Micah is flying home that day, and I have

to pick him up at the airport. I can try to come back for them, but if his flight is late, it could be a problem."

"Don't worry about it. I'll feed the boys lunch after the game, then bring them back to the ranch." That would also give him a chance to meet her son.

"Thanks. I'm sure they'd like that."

He studied her for a moment. The white-gold highlights in her hair glistened in the afternoon sun. Damn, he wanted to kiss her. But it didn't seem right. Not until after they had a chance to talk and to address the now-what questions they should have tackled after they'd made love.

"Since I won't get to take you out tonight, I'd still like to take you to Kalispell for dinner and a movie on Friday night."

"That sounds like a lot of fun. But I don't think that's a good idea."

"I know. You said that before. But think about it."

"I already have. More than you know. And to be perfectly honest, if I get emotionally involved with you, the only thing I can see happening is me ending up with a broken heart. And I've had more than my share of those already."

Ramon wanted to tell her not to worry, that he'd never hurt her. But at this point, he wasn't entirely sure he could make a promise like that—and keep it. Because she was right. They had two strikes against them already.

But miracles happened—on the ball field and in life. And crossing paths with Callie seemed like a miracle in and of itself.

"I'm not giving up on taking you out."

A slow smile stretched across her lips, and her blue eyes lit up. "Let's see what tomorrow brings."

That was good enough for him. Taking it step by step and one day at a time sounded like a good idea.

"I'll talk to you later."

She nodded. Then Ramon climbed into his SUV and drove back to town. He had a lot of things to do this afternoon, and some more thinking to do. But the first item on his list was to talk to his father's friend Ben. He had a feeling that the future of the ranch could depend on that.

Following the Saturday morning ballgame and lunch at the Joe's Burger Junction in town, Ramon stopped by the Johnsons' apartment to pick up the mail, then he drove the boys back to the ranch. As he'd suspected, his meeting with Ben had been very illuminating—and he needed to share what he'd learned about Adam Hastings with Callie and Alana.

He pulled into the yard just as Callie was parking her white Honda near the barn. Someone sat in the passenger seat, so he assumed she'd just arrived home from picking up Micah at the Kalispell airport. Apprehension—or maybe nervousness—shot up his spine.

"Hey," Mark said. "Callie's home with her son. Come on, Jess. Let's go meet him."

Ramon had that exact same thought, but he didn't want to look too eager. It hadn't been that long ago when he'd been a teenager and at that awkward stage, especially when it came to having to deal with adults. So he didn't want to come across as pushy or trying too hard.

Only problem was, his experience with teenagers didn't include sixteen-year-old whiz kids. Something told him they were a breed of their own.

Mark and Jesse had already reached Callie's car when Ramon shut off the ignition and got out of his. He took his time crossing the yard, watching as a small-boned boy with scruffy brown hair climbed from the Honda's passenger seat.

He wasn't sure what he'd expected to see when he first met Callie's son. A typical teenager, he supposed. A kid nearing adulthood with a smartphone in hand, earbuds in place and his attention on anything but the present.

But dang. Micah, with his freckled nose and frail stature, barely looked sixteen. And he could probably go days without shaving.

"Me and my brother are glad you're here," Mark said. "Want us to help you carry anything?"

"No," Micah said, looking a little uneasy about the younger boys' exuberance. "I didn't bring much. I can get it myself. But thanks." He opened the back passenger door and removed a bulging gray backpack and a black canvas tote bag.

"You're going to love it here," Jesse said. "There's all kinds of stuff to do."

Something told Ramon that Micah would be a lot more comfortable in a library than he would be on a ranch. But he kept his mouth shut as he continued a slow approach.

When Callie's gaze met his, she said, "Micah, I'd like you to meet my friend Ramon."

The boy reached out a slender arm and shook Ramon's hand. "It's nice to meet you, sir."

"Call me Ramon."

Micah glanced at his mother, then back at Ramon. If he suspected that the two of them might be more than friends, he didn't say.

"How long are you able to stay?" Ramon asked.

"Until next Sunday, I guess. I thought I'd better make sure my mom was okay." He stole a peek at her tummy, then looked at Ramon.

Okay, so he had a few notions about their friendship. But Ramon let it go at that.

"Come on," Mark said. "We'll show you to your

room, if that's okay with you. Me and my brother stayed in there until my sister got here."

"Sure." Micah nodded toward the house. "I may as well put my stuff away."

As the boys headed toward the porch, Mark and Jesse practically walked on air as they began telling Micah how glad they were that he was here and how much he was going to like the ranch. Micah didn't appear to be convinced. And neither was Ramon.

He looked at Callie and smiled. "I can see why you worry about him. He looks young for his age."

"I know. But he's what they call an old soul. He's astute when it comes to reading people. And he's got a lot of common sense, too."

"I hope Mark and Jesse don't drive him crazy."

"We talked about them on the way home. He's cool with younger kids—in small doses. I'll just make sure they respect his private time."

Before Ramon could respond, the screen door squeaked open, and Alana walked outside. She stepped off the porch, crossed the yard and approached them with a smile.

"I just had a little chat with Katie," she said. "I found her on the service porch, crying softly while putting a load of clothes in the washer."

"Oh no," Callie said. "What's wrong?"

"She's feeling overwhelmed, and not just because of her recent surgery. She's struggling financially, academically and emotionally."

"I offered to help out," Ramon said.

"She mentioned that, but it's not just the rent and groceries. What with the costs of her school, the boys' extracurricular activities and all of that, she's barely staying afloat, even when she had both jobs and two paychecks coming in. She also thinks Jesse needs a tutor, someone who specializes in kids with reading disabilities. She's afraid she'll have to withdraw from her classes and postpone her application to vet school."

Ramon understood. He'd had to give up his dream of playing in the major leagues, and even though he'd found another career, he still felt a pang of disappointment whenever he thought about what might have been. "I'd hate to see her drop out of school—even if it's just for a semester or two. It's hard to go back."

"I know." Alana smiled at Ramon, then turned to Callie. "That's why I invited her and the boys to live here. We have plenty of room. Right before Grandpa got his diagnosis, he'd fixed up that outbuilding for the foreman he'd planned to hire. It has a kitchenette, a bathroom and two bedrooms."

Ramon had noticed the new roof. He'd thought it was odd that Jack had made that repair before the others. But then he hadn't expected to die.

"And I can work with Jesse," Alana added. "I'm

not an expert by any means, but one of the kids I took care of had learning disabilities and needed a special tutor. I sat in on all of his sessions and learned ways for me to help him at home."

"That's great," Ramon said. "What'd Katie say when you offered your help?"

"She cried harder, but in a good way. She told me that she and the boys would help with chores. And since she's worked at the veterinary clinic, she knows a lot more about animals than I do."

"At least she knows which end of a cow to feed." Callie laughed and gave her friend a hug. "I love you. You're the best."

Alana, her eyes glistening with emotion, waved her off. "Please, how could I not invite them to stay?"

"I'm glad you did."

"Hey," Ramon said, "now that I have you both here, I need to tell you something. I've done a little research and found out that Adam Hastings is a Texas rancher looking to buy property in Montana and expand his holdings. In fact, he just made a sweet deal with Ellen Trapper to buy her place, which is just a few miles down the road."

"No kidding?" Alana furrowed her brow. "Ellen's lived on that property all her life."

"You know her?" Callie asked.

"I've only met her once before. At my grandfather's funeral. She went to school with my grandmother. From what I heard, she's been working that ranch ever since her husband died, so I guess she's tired and ready to do something different."

Maybe, Ramon thought. But something didn't seem right about a wealthy Texas rancher buying up Montana property. And what he found more bothersome was the fact that someone working for Hastings had checked with an area title company to find out if there were any liens against the local ranches.

It would appear that he was willing to acquire properties either by hook or crook. But why?

"Whoo-hoo!" one of the boys shouted as the screen door squeaked open.

Ramon glanced over his shoulder and watched as Mark dashed out of the house, Jesse on his heels, the screen slamming behind them. They hurried down the porch steps and across the yard.

Jesse pumped his fist and hollered, "Yee-haw!"

Apparently Katie had told them about the move, and they were both all in.

"Coach," Mark called out, his eyes sparkling, his excitement contagious. "Did you hear the good news? We don't have to go back to that dumb old apartment. Only to get our stuff."

"That's awesome. I'm happy for you."

"Can you believe it?" Jesse asked, a smile plastered across his face. "We're going to live here now. On Rancho Esperanza!"

Hope Ranch.

It appeared to be a fitting name change for what used to be the Lazy M, especially for those who lived here now. But holding on to the ranch, renovating it and making it productive wasn't going to be easy. And Adam Hastings seemed to be champing at the bit to either purchase or make some kind of claim on the property.

Ramon would do whatever he could to help Alana, but since Hastings hadn't made an illegal or threatening move, he couldn't do much yet. So until the guy showed his hand, he'd keep his concern to himself. There was no need to mention anything to Alana or Callie until he had more details—or had reason to worry about them.

Callie remained in the yard until Ramon drove away, his tires kicking up rocks and dust along the graveled road that led in and out of the ranch. She'd not only wanted him to meet Micah, but she'd also hoped to see them interact. Still, it was probably best that he left when he did. She needed some time to be alone with her son, to talk to him away from the others.

Ramon's car had barely disappeared from sight when Micah joined Callie in the yard. He'd gotten an inch or two taller since she'd last seen him, a sign that he was finally having a growth spurt that might help him catch up in size to the other boys his age.

She'd never felt awkward around her son, but she did today. So much had changed. And while she had plenty of reasons to be concerned—about him, about their mother/son relationship, the babies and the future—she offered him a no-worries smile. "Did you get settled in your room?"

"Yeah." He scanned the ranch, his brow furrowed, his hands on his hips. He'd looked a lot like his father when he was younger. But not so much anymore. Or maybe time had dulled her memory of the brilliant but rebellious teenager she'd once loved.

"The ranch is kind of cool," she said, hoping he'd approve of her move, that he'd feel comfortable while he was staying here, that he'd be eager to return.

When he didn't respond, she prodded him. "Don't you agree?"

"It's not what I expected."

"I know what you mean. There's a lot of work that needs to be done, but your aunt Alana has big plans for this place. Little by little we're fixing things up. And before you know it, it'll feel like home. Just wait and see."

"Yeah. Sure."

He clearly didn't believe her. But maybe the

run-down ranch wasn't the problem. Maybe his uneasiness ran deeper than that.

Did he feel out of place? He often did, especially when he was younger. And maybe even more so, now that he was in college with people several years older than him, adults who were stronger and much larger in frame.

When he'd been younger, he'd preferred to be at home, where it was just the two of them. Where they didn't have to worry about the outside world. And now it probably seemed to him as if they'd joined a commune.

"I'm sure you feel a little awkward," she said. "I mean, with so many people around."

He cut a glance at her, his brow still furrowed. "That's not a problem. I live in a dorm, remember?"

How could she forget? Her heart ached knowing he lived so far away and with people who weren't always kind. He'd been an oddity to some, a novelty to others. And at times, he'd been someone to tease, to bully.

"What's wrong?" she asked. "What's going through that precious mind of yours?"

"It's just that…" He paused, and his expression softened. Yet it was still difficult to read. Was he sad? Confused? "It's not this place. It's just that things are…different."

When he glanced at her baby bump, which

seemed to have doubled in size since his arrival just an hour ago, she realized what was troubling him. At least, some of it.

"I'm sorry," she said, even though change wasn't always bad. She'd spent her life looking out for him, trying to make things easier for them both. And now she'd complicated everything.

"Don't be sorry," he said. "It's not your fault. It's just… Never mind."

He was clearly struggling with how he was going to fit into her life, but telling her "never mind" wasn't going to make it any less important, any less hurtful—to him, to her.

"Just so you know," she said, "I'm happy about the babies. I didn't plan for it to happen, and I'll have to make adjustments. But that doesn't mean I'll love you any less. Or that I'll be any less invested in you and your dreams as I've always been."

"I know, Mom." He offered her a weak grin. "And I'm okay with you being pregnant. I'm just worried about your health. Twin births can be complicated. And I'm concerned about how you'll get by without me."

"Alana has always been there for me. And for you. I moved here to help her with the ranch, but I'm sure I can stay as long as I want. I'm actually thinking about selling the house. That'll give me some money to tide me over until the twins are old enough for preschool."

He nodded. "Okay, I guess you've thought it out."

"Well, not entirely. But I've got options." She slipped her arm around him, and he leaned into her embrace.

They stood like that for a while, silent yet connected. She'd been afraid she might be losing him. And that would devastate her.

She had another question for him, one she probably should hold on to for a while, but she couldn't stop from asking. "What did you think of Ramon?"

Micah shrugged. "He's okay, I guess. We didn't really talk. Why?"

"Just curious. He's become a good friend, and I hope that you'll grow to like him."

Micah drew away and looked her square in the eye. "Is he the father of the babies?"

"No. He's not. But…" Callie bit her tongue, unable to voice the rest of her thought but unable to stop it from crossing her mind. *No, Ramon isn't the father of the twins. But I wish he were.*

"But what?" Micah asked, his gaze intense.

She couldn't very well deny that she'd been about to say something. "Ramon would like to date me. What do you think about that?"

"That's up to you. What's holding you back?"

"My age. He's probably six or seven years

younger than me. And he doesn't have children. He's also a city councilman who's going to run for mayor in a few months."

"Does he care that you're older than he is?"

She slowly shook her head. "I'm sure he's thought about it, but apparently, it doesn't bother him. At least I don't think it does."

"Did you tell him about the babies?"

"Yes. Of course." She placed a hand on her growing belly. "I wouldn't be able to keep it a secret much longer."

Micah cocked his head. "And he still wants to go out with you?"

She nodded, realizing where he was going with his line of questioning. "I know what you're going to say. If it doesn't bother him, then why should it bother me?"

"Exactly."

Callie slipped both arms around her son and hugged him. "I knew your IQ was off the charts. I just didn't realize your emotional intelligence was, too."

"Yeah, well I didn't inherit all my genes from my father, Mom."

She couldn't help but smile. "Have I told you lately how much I love and admire you?"

"Yeah, in the car on the way here."

"Hmm. Good point. I just don't want you to ever forget it."

"I won't, Mom. Do you mind if I give you a bit of advice?"

"No, not at all."

"I don't want to see you hurt. So before you get too involved, make sure Ramon is a good man, and that he'll treat you right."

"I'm pretty sure already," she said.

"I hope you're right. Because if he mistreats you or lies to you…" He paused. "He'll have to answer to me."

Chapter Fourteen

By the time Ramon arrived at the Meadowlark Café, it was almost noon, and most of the tables had been taken. Instead of his usual spot near the window, he'd have to sit toward the front of the restaurant, which, fortunately, was usually assigned to Callie.

Speaking of Callie, she was serving lunch to two women and a child in one of the corner booths. She looked up, and when she noticed him, she smiled and mouthed, "I'll be right with you."

He acknowledged her words with a nod, then stopped briefly near the refrigerated display case to look over the pies and cakes they had today, even though he had no intention of having dessert.

Too bad, he thought. Gloria wasn't just a good cook, she was one hell of a baker, too.

Ramon took a seat at the open table and waited for Callie to stop by for his order. He didn't have to wait long.

"I didn't see you at breakfast." She pulled her pad and pen from her apron, which no longer did a good job of hiding her baby bump. "But then again, it's Monday. And you don't usually eat here."

"That's because I usually attend the Rotary Club meetings at the country club each week, remember? I ate there."

She blessed him with a smile, her blue eyes sparkling. "I thought you might have moved on to greener pastures."

"No other pastures for me." He tossed her a wink. "Not while you work here."

The door creaked open, and they both glanced up to see Leon Cunningham enter the eatery. The heavyset contractor in his midfifties was a braggart. He also had loose ties to Bryan Livingston, the councilman who'd been convicted of political corruption and fraud. And even though he'd managed to be the low bidder and land a few city jobs, no one had been able to actually tie him to the Livingston scandal.

From what Ramon had heard, Leon had expected to be the one appointed to fill Bryan's vacant seat on the council, only to learn that Ramon had been chosen over him.

"Does Leon come here often?" Ramon asked.

"Once in a while. Why?"

"No reason," he said. But that wasn't entirely true. Leon had tossed his hat in the ring and was now running against Ramon in the mayoral race. Leon didn't have much chance of winning, but either way, it seemed like a good idea to keep his eyes and ears open, especially with a man he didn't trust.

When Leon spotted Ramon, he made his way over to his table, reached out and shook hands. "How are you doing, Cruz? Ready to withdraw from the election?"

"Not yet. How about you?"

Leon chuckled. "I guess we're both in it to win it." Then he gave Callie the once-over, his eyes lingering longer than was polite. His gaze settled on her expanding waistline for a moment, then he tossed her a cocky grin. "How're you doing, honey?"

Ramon's gut clenched at Leon's good-ol'-boy attitude toward women—especially when it came to ogling Callie and calling her *honey.*

Then Leon glanced at Ramon. "I hear you've been spending a lot of time at this particular restaurant. And you always sit at a table that this pretty little lady serves. Makes me wonder if you're fond of more than just the food they serve at the Meadowlark Café."

"I'm not sure where you heard that. Sounds to me like it came from the rumor mill." Ramon sat back in his chair and crossed his arms. "I have better intel than that."

Leon chuckled. "Yeah, well, I do have my sources. And most are pretty damned accurate. But I'll let you get back to placing your order. I wouldn't want you to keep the pretty lady waiting."

If his unworthy opponent hadn't walked away, Ramon might have shown him to the door and kicked him to the curb. But he wasn't the kind to make a scene, especially in public.

"What a jerk," Callie said.

"You're telling me." Ramon figured the election was in the bag, but he couldn't be sure. And losing to a man like Leon Cunningham would be a bitter pill to swallow.

"So what'll you have?" Callie asked. "Today's special is meat loaf, roasted red potatoes and buttered green beans."

"I'd rather have something light. How about the Greek salad?"

"You got it."

Before Callie could turn away, Ramon reached out and caught her arm. "Did you give any thought to going out to dinner with me one night this week?"

"Actually, I did."

"And?"

She paused briefly, then offered him a dimpled smile. "Okay."

Excitement raced through him, warming him from the inside out and setting his hormones on edge.

"But I'm working the next couple of evenings," she added.

"How about Saturday night?"

"Sounds good."

It sounded damned good to him, too. Maybe too good. Because if his visceral reaction was any clue, he'd have to say that he was getting dangerously close to falling for the beautiful expectant mother. And that didn't seem to bother him a bit.

Up until today, Callie hadn't considered Leon Cunningham to be anything other than a local businessman and a customer. Of course, he'd never been one of her favorites—not by a long shot. Nevertheless, she'd always offered him a warm smile and a kind word. But when she'd stood by and heard him talk to Ramon, when he'd shown very little respect for either one of them, her opinion of him changed. Big-time.

Needless to say, she hadn't been in the mood to serve him or the two men who'd joined him shortly after he arrived. Fortunately, he'd taken a seat at one of Shannon's tables. Still, while Callie had done her best to ignore him, she couldn't ignore the fact that his stay at the restaurant had gone into overtime.

The lunch crowd, including Ramon, had already gone about their day, leaving the café nearly empty. And since Shannon had just served the jerk a slice of Gloria's four-layer fudge cake topped with a double scoop of vanilla ice cream, it didn't appear that he'd be leaving anytime soon.

She didn't recognize the two men with him. One was a fair-haired guy in his midthirties. The other was older—maybe fifty—and wore a business suit. She'd done her best to avoid their table for the past two hours, but she had to admit she wondered what they were talking about.

Since she no longer had anyone to serve and still had another hour to work, she began to clean up behind the counter, starting with the coffee maker.

Moments later, Shannon came up beside her and whispered, "I need to talk to you."

Shannon clearly didn't want anyone to overhear what she had to say, so Callie focused on the brown-stained carafe in her hand and lowered her own voice. "About what?"

"Those three dork-a-roos who've been sitting back there for the last couple of hours."

Callie stepped to her right and turned her back

to Shannon so the men didn't know they were being talked about.

"You know who the fat old guy is," Shannon said. "Right?"

Callie started to nod, then caught herself. "Leon Cunningham. And he's running for mayor. Against Ramon."

"I know. They've been bad-mouthing him. The younger guy said they could really do some political damage if they put the right spin on their story. Since you and Ramon are friends, I thought you should know. I was going to tell you later, but then your name came up."

Callie stiffened. "What'd they say?"

"That you look pregnant. And that you and Ramon have been seen together a lot. And not just here. Leon thinks you're having Ramon's baby. He also said, if you're as far along as you look, you must have gotten pregnant before Ramon's wife left town. He thinks that an affair caused the divorce."

"Oh my gosh. That's total BS."

"I know." Shannon let out a huff. "You're not even pregnant. Right?"

Bile rose in Callie's throat, but she swallowed it down. "Actually, I am. But not nearly as far along as that jerk thinks I am. I'm having twins."

"OMG. That's wild. What a trip." Shannon glanced at Callie's midsection, apparently so caught up in her own world that she was just now realizing what the apron had been hiding. When she looked up, her blue eyes, which she'd emphasized with today with a heavy coating of turquoise shadow and fake lashes, widened. "I mean, it's cool, though."

Callie might have found Shannon's reaction comical if she hadn't been so angry at Cunningham.

"Is Ramon the father?" Shannon asked. "I mean, dang. He's a good-looking guy, and he'd make gorgeous…" As if realizing she'd just stepped way out of bounds, Shannon flushed and slapped a hand over her mouth. "I'm really sorry, Callie. I mean, you've always been respectful of my personal life. I just… Well, it's none of my business."

No, it wasn't. It wasn't *anybody's*, and Callie had half a notion to march right over to Cunningham's table and give him a piece of her mind. But that would only make matters worse.

Instead, she placed a hand Shannon's shoulder. "Will you please keep this to yourself? All of it? The false accusations and assumptions those guys made, my pregnancy? This is bound to get ugly, and I need to figure out how to stop a conversation like that from going off the rails."

"Sure, Callie. I wouldn't do anything to hurt you."

Not purposely, anyway. Callie stole a glance

across the room, where Leon ate his dessert. Two women seated across from him whispered among themselves. Had they overheard the men's conversation? When they both looked at her, she got her answer.

Callie removed her apron. "Cover for me, okay? I need to get out of here."

"You got it."

The last thing in the world Callie wanted was for her personal life to get top billing when the town rumor mill began to churn out malicious gossip, especially while Micah was in town.

But some things couldn't be helped. This story, while completely false, would be too juicy to ignore. And when it hit the airwaves, Callie had reason to believe many of the good citizens of Fairborn would turn against the one man who could be the best mayor the town had ever had.

She needed to talk to Ramon, to let him know what was coming down the pike. At least that way, he'd be prepared to put out a few fires before Cunningham's mudslinging destroyed his campaign.

Ramon had just reached the Department of Public Works and stepped into the small lobby when his cell phone rang. He glanced at the screen, prepared to let it roll over to voice mail and to shut off the ringer. But when he saw who was calling, he answered quickly. "Hey, Callie. I'm just about to walk into a meeting. Can I call you back?"

"I don't think this can wait. I'll make it quick."

As she told him what had gone down at the café, what Leon Cunningham planned to do, the rumors and false innuendos he intended to make, Ramon's gut tightened. It took all he had not to drive back to the café and confront his opponent.

As it was, he walked outdoors, needing fresh air—and privacy so he could speak freely. "I'm so sorry, Callie. I had no idea you'd get sucked into something like this."

"I know. This wasn't what either of us expected, but it's going down. And you need to be prepared."

"What about you?"

She paused for a couple of beats. "I won't lie. This really stinks. But I'm more worried about you. I know how much this campaign means to you."

Ramon pressed the cell phone tight against his ear. "You mean more to me than the campaign. I'd withdraw before I'd let your name get dragged through the dirt. But I don't want to see a man like Cunningham get elected. Fairborn needs an honest leader and not another corrupt politician."

She blew out a sigh. Was it in resignation? Disbelief?

"Under the circumstances," she said, "I'm not going out to dinner with you. And I think you'd better start eating at a different restaurant from now on."

She was probably right. But he wanted to spend a special evening with her. And he liked seeing her every day.

In some ways, Cunningham's claims hit a little too close for comfort because, even though Ramon wasn't the father of Callie's twins, he wished he was.

"Listen," he said, "I have to go. But I'm coming by the ranch tonight. We can talk more then."

"I don't think that's a good idea."

Ramon wasn't going to take no for an answer. "I'll see you after six. But don't fix dinner for me. I'll eat before I get there."

Then he disconnected before she could object.

Considering that Callie had worked the morning shift, she arrived at the ranch earlier than usual. Alana's car was parked near the barn, so she assumed Mark and Jesse were home from school. She entered the house through the back door and headed to the kitchen, where the boys sat at the kitchen table, munching on orange wedges and apple slices and doing their homework.

Alana, who'd been overseeing their work, glanced up and smiled. "Hi, Cal. You're home early."

"Things were slow today, so I left." She scanned

the small, outdated but tidy kitchen. "Where's Micah?"

"He was helping Katie with her calculus when we got back from school. She got behind while she was sick and has been struggling to catch up. But he's probably in his room now and on his laptop. Did you know he plans to take a couple of online classes this summer?"

"Yes, he told me. And I wasn't surprised." Callie hooked the shoulder strap of her purse on the back of a chair. "He's always researching or reading something. I really wish he'd loosen up a little. He's never been one to play, but I think it would do him some good."

"I agree." Alana brightened. "Maybe we can plan a game night." She paused and bit down on her bottom lip. "Come to think of it, there's only a deck of playing cards and a cribbage board here. I wonder if I can purchase some used games at the thrift store next to Tip Top Market."

The last thing Callie wanted to do, especially after the day she'd had, was to play games. She nodded toward the back door. "Can I talk to you outside for a minute?"

Alana sobered, picking up on Callie's troubled vibes. "Sure. I'll be back, boys."

Moments later they were in the yard.

"What's up?" Alana asked.

Callie repeated the story. "And apparently, since

I appear to be further along in my pregnancy, Cunningham is suggesting that Ramon and I were messing around while he was still married, and that's why his wife left."

"That's awful. What a horrible man."

"I know. I'm so new in town that people don't really know me well enough to realize I'd never be a home wrecker. Heck, Alana, all you and I have ever wanted in life is to have a family of our own. And that doesn't mean snatching someone else's husband."

"You've got that right. I've had enough hand-me-downs in my life. And so have you. Besides, you, of all people, deserve happiness, not to mention romance."

"You do, too."

Neither of them needed to say it. Or to be reminded. But they'd both spent their early years in dysfunctional homes with alcoholic or drug-addicted parents. And they'd been lucky to come out of it virtually unscathed. So to speak.

"Everything eventually worked out for us," Callie said. "And I'm sure this will work out, too. At least, in the long run. It just hurts. I hate to admit this, but I love Ramon. And it's going to kill me to see him in town as I do my best to pretend I don't feel anything for him."

"Then don't pretend," Alana said. "Who cares what people might say?"

"I care. It's not just my reputation on the line. It's Ramon's. And he's got an upcoming election to worry about."

"True." Alana blew out a sigh.

Callie would do whatever it took to protect Ramon from the gossip that could hurt his campaign. She'd have to protect herself, too. She'd always hated being in the spotlight. And in this case, she was sure to fall short of everyone's expectations, especially when it came to being the kind of woman the hometown hero deserved.

"Maybe," Alana said, "after the election, and when the rumor dies down, the two of you can date."

"If he's still interested in me." Callie looked at her best friend. "Tell me that I'm making the right decision by cutting all ties with him, at least for the time being."

"I'm the last one in the world who should give romantic advice to anyone."

"That's not true," Callie said. "You're the only one I can trust, the only one who's honest enough to tell me how it is."

"I'm a doofus when it comes to relationships. I've never had one work out. And…" Alana chuffed. "You're not going to believe this, but I'm still kicking myself for running out on Clay when we met in Colorado. And the sad thing is, I don't even know his last name."

Callie gave her friend a hug. "You'll meet someone else one of these days. The right guy. And this mess with Ramon will work out, too. It has to. And on the bright side, at least we have each other."

"Not to mention two precious babies who'll have the best mommy and godmother ever."

Where would Callie be if she didn't have Alana? Lost, it would seem.

Alana was the ultimate best friend forever. Only thing was, Callie had a pretty good idea that Ramon might have given her a run for her money in the BFF category. But that's as far as it would go. Romance was out of the question, because, at this point in time, the only thing she could expect from pursuing a relationship like that was to be a part of destroying the man she loved. And she'd never allow that to happen, even if she had to be the one who walked away first.

Chapter Fifteen

After dinner, Callie cleared the kitchen table and filled the sink with warm, soapy water. After what had happened in town, she felt as grungy as the dishes in the sink.

Katie had already excused herself to polish the paper she'd been working on all afternoon, while Micah planned to help Mark with his science project.

"I'll be back in a minute," Alana said. "I'll get a box of art supplies I have left over from my nanny days in Texas."

"Cool," Micah said, as he and Mark went to the mudroom to get the project they'd created this morning and left near the window to dry.

"Can I help you guys?" Jesse asked his older brother.

Callie smiled. Jesse didn't get left behind often, and this time it had been his choice.

"I thought you didn't like doing homework," Mark said. "You wanted to go outside and play with Rascal and Chewie instead of helping this morning."

"I know, but I thought you guys were doing dumb stuff, like math and spelling. I didn't know you were going to make a *volcano*."

If Callie hadn't needed to open the café this morning, she would have loved watching Micah help Mark with his project. The boys had first made a batch of dough and formed it around a plastic soda bottle. And now that it was dry, they were going to paint it.

After Micah set the homemade volcano on the table, he reached over and placed his hand on Jesse's shoulder. "You can watch, buddy. Maybe you'll learn something."

Callie was more interested in watching Micah interact with the younger boys than finishing the dishes. So she rinsed the plate she'd just washed and placed it in the drainer. Then she shut off the water and let the rest of the dishes soak for a moment. As she dried her hands, she remained by the sink and observed the boys' activity from a distance.

Jesse pulled out a chair, knelt on the seat, leaned forward and studied the white glob that rested on a square piece of cardboard. "I think volcanoes are cool. And now Mark can show his class what they look like."

"I'm going to show them how it erupts, too," Mark said.

"Really?" Jesse's eyes grew wide. "With *fire* and hot *lava*?"

Micah smiled. "The bottle is filled with water, red food coloring and soap. Now that the dough is dry, we're going to paint it to look like a volcano on the outside. Then, after Mark gives his report, he's going to add baking soda to the bottle, and when he pours in the vinegar, it'll blow."

The same thing had happened today at the café. Leon poured in the vinegar when he'd made assumptions that weren't true and spread those lies for all the town to hear, and any hope Callie'd once had for her and Ramon's relationship had blown sky high.

"But I don't get it," Jesse said. "How's that supposed to work? Don't you have to heat it up or set it on fire?"

"Nope." Micah smiled at the inquisitive younger boy. "When you mix baking soda and vinegar together, it produces carbon dioxide gas that's going to bubble up with the help of the detergent. And that'll force the fake lava to erupt."

Ka-boom. Her thoughts drifted to Leon's lies, which were bubbling up and erupting, threatening to ruin everything in their path.

But she would think about Leon later. Right now, she wanted to focus on her son and how he seemed to be finding a place at the ranch. Did he have any idea how much she loved him? Did he realize that he was still—and always would be—an important and integral part of her new life, that nothing would ever change that? He might live on campus and only be spending the week and the upcoming summer with her, but he'd always be her son, her pride and joy.

She was so glad he was here with her, especially now. Having him home, even if it was only for a few more days, would help take her mind off her loss. It already hurt like the devil, and she hadn't even told Ramon they could no longer be friends, let alone lovers.

Alana returned to the kitchen with a small box and placed it on the table, next to the volcano. "Here's the paint and brushes."

"These colors are perfect," Mark said. "Black, brown, red and white."

Alana left the boys to their work and joined Callie at the sink. Then she picked up a dish towel and pulled the wet dinner plate from the drainer. They worked in silence for a while, then Alana lowered her voice and asked, "What did you decide? Are you going to take some time off from the diner until things settle down in town?"

Callie had mentioned this possibility while the two of them had fixed dinner earlier, but she'd had second thoughts since then. "I decided against it. No matter when I go back to town, I'll have to face the whispers and the rumors. So I may as well get it over with. Things will eventually die down, and then I can get on with life."

"You're probably right, but I hate that you have to deal with that crap. Besides, you have no reason to feel any shame or guilt."

"Mom," Micah said, "if you're going to work at the café tomorrow, I'm going with you."

Apparently, Callie and Alana hadn't spoken as quietly as they'd hoped.

"You don't need to do that," Callie said. "I'll be fine, honey."

"I know *you* will. But *I* won't be unless I hang out with you and see for myself. That's why I came to visit this week, remember?"

Callie loved that boy, now more than ever. But he couldn't protect her from the fallout of Leon Cunningham's gossip. No one could. She had a feeling that ending things with Ramon wasn't even going to be enough to keep her from becoming fodder for the rumor mill. After all, she *was* pregnant, she *wasn't* married and the babies' father was so far removed from her life that he'd be little more than a myth.

Unfortunately, Leon's lies could easily tarnish Ramon's standing in the community. And assuming the majority of the voters believed the rumors he and his cronies stirred up, the town would take the ultimate hit if Leon became mayor. For that reason, Callie's mind was set, her decision made. She'd cut all ties with Ramon. Not doing so would be too risky for everyone involved.

And as for the future?

That was left to be seen, but she doubted time would be her ally when it came to renewing their relationship. Her life was only going to become more complicated. And, as a result, other women were going to be far more attractive to him.

So there was no way he'd remain single for long. And she'd be okay with that. She'd have to be.

The doorbell rang, and her heart jumped, taking a soaring leap before belly flopping into the pit of her stomach. That must be Ramon. It had to be. She had no idea what he'd say, but her mind was set, her words already formed.

He might agree to take a break for the time being and assume they'd get together again after the election. But Callie knew that wasn't going to happen. Their so-called friendship and bittersweet romance were over for good.

* * *

Ramon stood on the front porch, waiting for someone to answer the bell and invite him into the house. He expected that person to be one of the Johnson boys, although he hoped it would be Callie. He wanted to talk to her. They needed to put their heads together to come up with a game plan that would help them deal with the unexpected turn of events that Leon had forced on them.

But more than that, he needed to see her, to hear her voice. Whenever he'd had a troubling or difficult day, she had a way of righting his world. And today had been one of the worst he'd ever had, especially since the gossip had begun to spread.

Late this afternoon, he'd had a chat with Brandon Dodd, the Fairborn deputy sheriff. Ramon had let him know about the lies Leon was spreading, the mudslinging, but mostly he'd wanted to share his suspicion about Leon's ties to Bryan Livingston and the political corruption that had rocked the town last year. Those ties seemed to be even stronger now. Brandon had agreed and said he'd had similar thoughts and would check into it.

Now Ramon waited on the front porch, listening to approaching footsteps from inside the house. A smile stretched across his face as the door swung open and he spotted Callie. His heart warmed and, even though the sun had set, his day brightened. That was, until he noted the sober expression she wore.

His smile faded in the evening air, and his brow furrowed. "What's the matter?"

"Nothing. Not really."

Um. Yeah. Something was definitely wrong.

When she remained standing in the doorway without opening the screen and stepping aside, without inviting him in, he realized that whatever the something was, it was worse than he'd thought.

She glanced over her shoulder, as if checking to make sure no one was behind her, that no one could hear what she was about to say. Apparently, she didn't see anyone, because she lowered her voice and said, "This thing we had, whatever it was, isn't going to work. Not in the foreseeable future. There's too much standing in the way."

"Temporarily, maybe. But it's nothing we can't work out."

"I'm not even sure about that. You're going to make an awesome mayor, and the town needs you."

"What if I need *you*?" The words rolled out of his mouth in spite of his hesitancy to say them in the past. But they were true.

She seemed to soften her stance, but just for a moment. "You might have needed me for a while. And I'll admit that I needed you, too. We'd both been recovering from bad relationships. What we shared was the first step we made to start dating again, to move on to something better."

She had a point. They'd both been rebounding—

her from a guy who'd left her pregnant and him from a wife who'd filed for divorce and never looked back. Was Callie right?

Doubt flickered, but only for a moment. "You don't really believe that, Callie. Not after that Saturday afternoon."

Again, she glanced over her shoulder, then her gaze returned to him. "It was just sex. We both needed it, and it was good. It was great, actually. But don't put too much thought into it. I didn't."

Her dismissal of what they'd done, what they'd had, struck like a stab to the gut. Seriously?

No, he thought. She couldn't be this cold about what they'd shared. There was no way she'd just blown it off. No way she hadn't thought about it. Or that she hadn't been moved by it.

"I don't believe you," he said.

She stiffened, locking the latch on the screen, using the door as a shield between them. "I'm not sure what I believe right now, other than we need to make a clean break from each other and let the talk die down. Maybe, after the election, we can see how we each feel, but for now, I think it's best if you go home."

Her words slammed into him, cracking his chest wide-open. This couldn't be happening. But it was.

"I'll go," he said, "but I want you to know that I feel a hell of a lot more than friendship for you. Sex between us wasn't just a release. It really meant something. And you weren't a transition, a stepping-stone until someone better came along."

Her lip twitched, and she gripped the edge of the door. But she still didn't open it, didn't let him in.

He couldn't force the issue—nor could he force his way inside. But neither could he just give up and walk away.

"I'm going to drop out of the mayoral election," he said.

At that, her expression changed, revealing a chink in her armor. "No way. That's crazy. What would happen to Fairborn if Leon became mayor?"

He flinched at the very thought. "The town would suffer." He had no doubt about that.

But hearing her say it triggered another thought. Was Callie taking a hit for the town? Was that why she claimed making love hadn't meant anything to her?

For once, he wasn't at all sure about anything. But he'd always been one to take the power position. "Are you doing this for me? For the town? You don't have to worry. I've got this."

"So do I." Then she shut the door.

She'd left him no choice but to walk away. As he returned to his car, his heart ached—worse than when Jillian left. Much worse. No freakin' comparison. Even though he and Jillian had been married for years.

What did it all mean?

He had no idea what he'd end up doing about Callie, about the pain he felt when she'd slammed the door, but for now, he was going to talk to the best friend and adviser he'd ever had.

Twenty minutes later, Ramon arrived at the place he still considered home. He'd called his dad a few minutes ago, letting him know that he was on his way over to talk. The ranch was pretty remote, and the rifle that hung over the mantel was always locked and loaded.

When Ramon opened the front door, he called out, "It's me."

"I'm in the kitchen. You hungry? I've got corn bread in the oven. It'll be done in a few minutes. And I just fixed a pot of chili."

Even if he was hungry and hadn't eaten in town, his dad's spicy chili was the last thing his stomach could handle. Not after Callie had kicked him to the curb.

"I'll pass," Ramon said as he scanned the small kitchen with its outdated yellow tile countertops and brown appliances. The only thing adorning the beige walls was a plaque that held the plastic singing fish one of his dad's buddies had given him as a gag gift.

His dad stood at the stove, his back to the doorway. "I've got news for you."

As far as Ramon was concerned, his own news was the only thing that mattered. But they had all night to talk about that, he supposed.

"I heard that guy from Texas just purchased the Trapper ranch," Dad said. "It's going into escrow on Monday."

"Oh yeah?" Now that Hastings had found another property in the area, would he back off and leave Alana alone? Ramon certainly hoped he would, but something told him that wouldn't be the case.

"You want a beer?" Dad asked.

"Yeah. That might help."

His dad started for the fridge, then stopped in his tracks to study Ramon. "What's bothering you, son? By that look on your face, I'd say someone kicked your dog."

"They actually kicked me." Ramon told him what was going on in town, what rumors his political opponent was spreading—and worse, how those lies had hurt the woman he'd come to care for. And how she'd ended things between them this evening.

The woman he *cared for*? Would it hurt this badly if that's all he felt for her?

Dad retrieved two long-neck bottles with twist-off tops from the fridge and handed one to Ramon, keeping the other for himself. "Callie sure is pretty. And she's smart."

That she was. Ramon twisted off the cap to his beer and took a long swig.

"I take it you love her," his dad said.

"I think so." Hell, who was he kidding? "I must love her, because it felt like a kick to the gut when she told me to leave."

"Does she love you?"

Ramon shrugged. "I'm not sure. Maybe, but if she does, she won't admit it. I have a feeling she's trying to save my political career, not to mention the whole damned town."

Oddly enough, his ex-wife hadn't felt the same way.

Your sports teams, your buddies and your dad always come first. And now that you've been appointed to fill that damned council seat, even the town has come between us.

"So Callie is loyal and considerate, huh? Ready to lay down her heart for her friend? If that's the case, then I'd say she's a keeper."

"I think so, too. But she ended things tonight, and I don't know what to do about it, how to fix it."

"I'm an expert on heartbreak—and on being able to live after the fact, protecting myself from further damage."

Ramon let out a ragged breath. "I think I'm following in your footsteps."

"Maybe you are, son. After your mom left us, I was crushed. And I spent years avoiding serious relationships. But I've been lonely when it comes to female companionship. In fact, I've been seeing Helena again. I think I might be ready to make the commitment she'd wanted from me."

"Now that's a surprise." Ramon took another sip of his beer.

"I'm happier when I'm with her."

"Then I'm happy for you."

"Thanks." Dad returned to the counter, picked up a couple of pot holders, opened the oven and pulled out the corn bread. He set it on the counter to cool.

When his father returned to his seat at the table, he asked, "So what are you going to do?"

"Callie took the decision out of my hands. She's cutting all ties to me until after the election."

"She's probably right. But is that what you want?"

He didn't answer, just picked at the beer label.

"Things will work out in the end, but the important thing is to win the election. Otherwise, Cunningham and his cronies will ruin this town."

Ramon took another swig of beer, wishing he could argue otherwise.

"You sure you don't want some chili?" Dad asked as he put a ladle in the pot and filled a bowl.

"Yeah, I'm sure."

After grabbing a spoon, his dad placed his bowl

on the table, then returned to the counter to cut a piece of corn bread.

Ramon only stayed long enough to finish his beer.

As he drove back to his house in town, he thought about what Callie had said, what she'd claimed.

She'd been wrong when she'd said they'd only had sex. It had been more than that. They'd made love. And there were strong feelings involved, even if both of them had been reluctant to admit it.

And that made things tough, because when all was said and done, Callie was the one Ramon wanted to run to when his world was falling apart. And today, when she'd made him choose the town over her, his world had been blown to smithereens.

He'd go along with her decision, but somehow, he had to figure out a way to keep her—and, at the same time, to save Fairborn from corruption.

Could he do it?

Chapter Sixteen

Micah had been tagging along to work with Callie for the past two days, coincidentally choosing the table near the window, where Ramon used to sit. Then he'd open up his laptop and work on one class assignment or another.

Callie had tried to assure him that the whispers, stares and occasional snooty looks didn't bother her, even though they did. But she'd shaken it off the best she could. Only trouble was, the Meadowlark Café had seen a big drop in business ever since Leon opened his big mouth.

Thankfully, Ramon hadn't come here to eat, which would have really set tongues wagging.

Still, if Callie's presence was causing the locals to avoid the diner, it might be best if she turned in her apron and order pad. Jasmine didn't deserve to lose business because of her employee's troubles.

So Callie's plan was to give her notice. She was prepared to stick it out for two weeks or more, depending on Jasmine's preference. In the meantime, she'd call a Realtor and put her Texas house on the market. The proceeds from the sale would allow her to get by for a couple of years. That way, she could remain at the ranch and devote her time to getting ready for the babies and helping Alana plant a garden and clean up the orchard.

When the front door opened, she looked up, hoping it was a customer, but it was only Shannon, arriving early for her shift. The young woman hadn't worked yesterday, and she wasn't due to come in today for another thirty minutes. After tossing her purse and backpack on the shelf under the register, Shannon grabbed a clean apron from the hook near the refrigerator display case that was jam-packed with desserts, since there'd been fewer customers than expected.

Shannon approached Callie, the spiky tips of her short black hair colored green today. "How's it going? Are you holding up okay?"

Callie mustered her best no-worries smile. "Yes, I'm doing fine."

"Good. If someone gives you any grief while I'm here, I've got your back."

"I appreciate that."

As Shannon tied the apron around her waist, she must have noticed Micah sitting alone. Even though he'd barely looked up when she walked in and had returned his focus to the laptop screen, she approached his table. "Hey. I haven't seen you before. Are you new in town?"

He shrugged. "Not exactly. My mom lives here, and I'm just visiting."

"Oh yeah? Who's your mom?"

"Callie."

Shannon's eyes grew wide, and a smile dimpled her cheeks. "No kidding? You're so lucky. Callie's awesome."

"Yeah, I think so."

Shannon's praise placed a balm on Callie's ragged heart. Still, she continued to work, pretending she wasn't eavesdropping on their conversation.

"What are you doing?" Shannon asked.

"Working on a project for an online course."

"Oh yeah? I'm taking classes, too. Where do you go to school?"

"Baylor University. In Texas."

"Whoa!" Shannon slapped her hands on her hips. "You're in college?"

Micah shrugged, and Callie flinched. The kid

had dealt with reactions like that all his life. It wasn't easy being different. And it wasn't easy for his mom, either.

"You must be super smart," Shannon said.

Again, the poor kid shrugged.

"Want to hang out sometime? I mean, while you're in town."

"I don't know. I'm staying out at the ranch and all. And I don't have a car."

"You can catch a ride to town with your mom. I don't have a car, either. So I do a lot of walking."

When Micah looked at Callie, his genius-caught-in-the-headlights expression said it all. *What's going on here? What am I supposed to say or do?*

Other than the occasional study group, Micah hadn't socialized much, and even then, he seemed happier to study on his own.

Callie knew she had to let her son figure this kind of thing out on his own. It was part of finding a real friend—and becoming one in return. But she couldn't help saying, "I'd be happy to drive you someplace." If he'd agreed to get a driver's license on his birthday, something he'd had no interest in doing, she would have let him use her car. She'd have to bring it up to him again tonight.

"So what do you say?" Shannon asked.

Micah thought about it for a couple of beats, then shrugged. "Sure. Why not?"

Callie blew out a soft sigh of relief. That was, until the door opened and a group of chattering people entered the café. She turned to greet them, but her welcoming smile vanished the moment she spotted Leon Cunningham bringing up the rear and herding the others inside. Her cheeks warmed, and bile churned in her stomach.

There had to be at least ten of Leon's cronies, including a redhead in her early forties Callie recognized as a reporter for the *Fairborn Gazette*.

"We're having a campaign meeting here," Leon said as he zeroed in on Callie. "Would you pull a few of those tables together?"

"Sure," Callie said.

Before she could take a step, Leon lifted up both his hands. "Hold on, honey. That was thoughtless of me. You shouldn't lug heavy tables and chairs around in your condition."

Callie saw red. "No worries, Leon. If I weren't fit and healthy, it could be a problem." She made a point of zeroing in on his belly, which lopped over his belt. "But I'm strong and capable of moving furniture. You, on the other hand, could hurt yourself."

One of his cronies chuckled, and Leon glared at Callie.

"I'll move the tables," Shannon said.

Leon scanned the nearly empty dining room, his eyes landing on Micah. "Is that your other fatherless kid? Rumor has it this isn't the only time you've been pregnant without a ring on your finger." He jerked his chin at her son. "Hey, son. You'd better move away from there. That table's reserved for Councilman Cruz, your mama's latest boyfriend."

Several people chuckled, their eyes bright. Suggestive.

"That's right, kid," the vocal crony added. "Take your video game and find another seat."

"He's not moving," Callie said. "No one owns that seat. Not even you, Mr. Cunningham."

"Well, now." Leon eyed her carefully. "Don't you have spunk for a woman who broke up our newest councilman's marriage?"

At that, Micah, who stood about five foot four and weighed all of 110 pounds, shoved back his chair, got to his feet and strode up to Leon, holding a glass of water, and threw it at the man. "That's a lie."

The crowd gasped. Callie did, too. Only she was filled with pride and wanted to shout, *You go, Micah.*

Leon wiped his face, then placed a meaty hand on Micah's chest and gave him a shove. Micah stumbled back and fell into a chair.

Before Callie could utter a word, Shannon jumped into what appeared to be the start of a fray. "You leave him alone. You just assaulted him."

"He charged me first. Besides, what do you know about the law, sweetie?" Leon asked her. "Keep out of this."

"I got an A in my criminal justice class," Shannon said.

Callie pulled Micah aside and, with a smile shining with pride planted across her face, pointed for him to return to his seat. Man, she loved that kid.

She turned to Leon. "You just assaulted a minor. And that's even worse. I have a good mind to press charges."

Gloria, with her wild, bleached-blond hair, rushed out of the kitchen like Thor, a meat tenderizer held up in her hand. "What the hell are you doing, Leon? Now you gotta bully kids?"

Leon raised both hands. "Now, now, Gloria. Put down that weapon. It's just a little misunderstanding. Chill. Nothing's going on here."

"Like heck it isn't," Gloria said. "I saw you push the kid. If you don't get out of my restaurant, I'm going to get the sheriff."

Leon chuffed. "You're just as bossy now as you were in grade school."

"And you're still a jerk who likes to pick on people to make you feel big."

Leon glared at Gloria. In a low tone, he said, "You don't own the place, even if you act like it most of the time."

"Actually, Jasmine just accepted my offer to buy it. You leaving now?"

When Leon didn't move, she strode to the door, meat tenderizer in hand. "I'll be back with Sheriff Dodd. You just assaulted a minor."

She'd no more than stepped outside when Ramon walked in wearing his trademark smile. When he spotted Leon, his ruddy face dripping wet, and then the gathered crowd, he sobered.

"What's going on?" Ramon's gaze sought out Callie, and her heart took off like a misfired shot, ricocheting this way and that.

What was he doing here? Hadn't he listened to a thing she'd told him? But dang, was she glad to see him.

As Ramon stared down Leon, the bully slunk back and his cronies began to disperse.

It seemed he'd come to her rescue until the journalist lifted her cell phone and snapped a picture. The gorgeous town councilman might be able to stop a woman dead in her tracks, but he couldn't stop the media storm that was about to hit.

Ramon's heart sank when he spotted Callie, her eyes leery, her cheeks flushed. She was his primary concern—his only one—as he scanned the room. A crowd had gathered at the Meadowlark Café, and not a very friendly one. Leon stood front and center, clearly the ringleader.

Micah stood off to the side, an empty water glass in his hand, his cheeks as bright as a vine-ripe tomato. He watched both Leon and Ramon like a wary hawk.

"Well, I'll be damned." Leon smirked. "Look who's here. *Again*." He shot a glance at Callie, his gaze drifting to her belly, and she placed her hands on the bump, as if she could hide it from sight.

Ramon's arms remained at his side, muscles flexed, hands clenched into fists. What he wouldn't give to plant a punch right into Leon's smug face. But he wasn't going to make a scene. At least, not any worse than what had already gone down.

He spotted Vera McDonald in the crowd, her cell phone lifted. "You looking for a story?" he asked the reporter.

"Always."

"Then I'll give you the straight scoop. And we can clear up the rumors right here, right now. Callie and I began seeing each other *after* my *ex*-wife left town. She's pregnant—with twins. And I intend to marry her—if she'll have me—and be a father to all three of her kids." He shot a glance at Callie, whose expression morphed from a worried frown to a faint smile, and his pulse spiked in a good way.

As much as he wanted to go to her, to slip his arms around her and offer comfort and support, he remained planted, waiting for Leon to make a move.

Leon narrowed his eyes and pointed a finger at Ramon. "If you expect to be elected mayor in this town, you'd better cull out your choice of friends."

"You'd better take your own advice," Ramon told him. "Because if being involved with the sweetest and kindest woman in Fairborn causes me to lose the election, then so be it."

Leon chuffed and turned toward the door.

Before he could exit, Sheriff Dodd entered with Gloria on his tail, a hammer of some kind in her hand.

"I'm not sure what's happening here," Dodd told Leon, "but I'm tired of hearing about you slandering anyone who crosses your path. I'm going to have to ask you to leave."

Leon stood his ground. "I'll go. For now. You haven't seen the last of me yet."

"That's for sure," the sheriff said. "There's a grand jury inquiry coming down the road, and your dealings and your connections to Bryan Livingston are going to come to light. You might want to reconsider running for a leadership position in town."

"Lies. All lies." As Leon stomped off, his cronies followed him out the door, but once outside, they went in different directions. Apparently, they wanted to cut their own connections to Leon.

However, Vera McDonald, the reporter, lagged behind and approached Ramon and Callie, her cell phone still in hand. "I want you both to know that I won't be using any of the photos I took today. And the only story I'll be working on now is that grand jury inquiry."

"Thanks, Vera." Ramon opened his arms for Callie, not sure if she'd step into his embrace. When she did, his heart soared. "We appreciate that."

As Vera headed toward the door, Gloria took Brandon aside and led him to a stool at the counter. "Have a seat, Sheriff. I'm going to pour you a cup of coffee and serve you a big slice of apple pie. I just pulled it out of the oven, so it's still hot. And don't bother reaching for your wallet. It's on the house."

The dark-haired law enforcement officer winked at the cook. "Will that pie come with a scoop of vanilla ice cream?"

"Two of 'em," Gloria said as she disappeared into the kitchen.

Now that tempers had cooled and things at the Meadowlark Café had gone back to normal, Ramon could finally tell Callie what he'd come to say before he'd stumbled upon Leon's ruckus.

She looked up at him, her blue eyes as bright as the Montana sky, and smiled. "After telling you to stay away last night, I didn't expect to see you today. But I'm glad you came, especially when you did."

"I couldn't stay away. I love you, Callie. And I

hope you feel the same way about me. But even if you're not sure about that yet, I'm willing to wait. How can I convince you that I love you, that we're meant to be together?"

"It's not going to take much to convince me of that, especially after you claimed me, Micah and the babies without batting an eye." She turned to face him. "I love you, too."

His heart damn near shot out of his chest. He drew her close and kissed her, a prequel to the many he planned to give her later tonight.

When the kiss ended, he hated to let her go, but they had an audience. Reluctantly, he released her. As he tucked a loose strand of hair behind her ear, he broke into a smile that couldn't possibly tell her how very happy he was.

"Honey," he said, "I've been dying to take you out to dinner for the longest time, and you keep putting me off. But I'm no quitter. How about tonight?"

Before Callie could answer, Micah walked up to them and reached out his hand to Ramon. "Thank you for stepping up and defending my mom. Besides me, she's never had anyone do that before."

Ramon gave the boy's hand a firm shake. "I'd defend her with my life. And you, too, Micah."

His cheeks flushed, and he glanced down at his feet for a moment. Then he looked up and smiled. "Thanks. That's good to know."

"You might not be into baseball," Ramon said,

"but you're welcome to come watch any of our Little League games. And when it's over, I'll spring for pizza."

"Sure. I'd like that. It'd be cool to see Mark and Jesse play." Micah turned to Callie. "If you don't mind driving home alone, Mom, I'm going to stick around the café after you get off work." He nodded at Shannon, who had begun to mop the wet floor. "We were talking before that jerk came in, and I told her I'd help bus tables and stuff so she can leave sooner. Then, after the diner closes, we're going to a movie. She'll have one of her friends drop me off at the ranch when it's over."

"I don't mind at all." Callie's bright smile dimpled her cheeks. "I like Shannon. She has a kind heart. And she knows how to have fun. She'll be a good friend for you."

"Yeah, I think so, too." Micah took a step backward, then turned and headed back to his table, where he began to shut down his laptop.

Ramon winked at Callie, then led her to a quiet corner, out of everyone's view. "Now, where were we?"

She smiled and returned to his arms. "You'd just asked me out to dinner tonight, and I was about to say yes."

He pressed a kiss on her brow. "That's just what I'd hoped to hear."

"There's something I want you to know," she

said, her voice so whisper soft that it sent tingles up his back to his neck. "I realize that, in the heat of the moment, you claimed that the twins are yours. And as much as I appreciate it, I won't hold you to it."

"You'd *better*. I'm not like other politicians. I don't make promises or claims that I don't intend to keep." He brushed his lips across hers. "And as for the upcoming election, if you feel the least bit uncomfortable standing beside me during my campaign, I'll remove my name from the ballot. You mean more to me than anything."

"Don't you dare withdraw from the race." She lifted her index finger, poked his chest and grinned. "This town needs you. And the election's going to be a slam dunk."

Ramon captured her hand, turned it over and kissed her palm. "Maybe. Maybe not. But either way, I'm already a winner because I have you by my side."

And that was true. He and Callie had become more then friends, more than lovers. They were a team, and together, they'd tackle any trouble that came their way.

Today.

Tomorrow.

And always.

* * * * *

Look for Alana's story,
Their Night to Remember,
the next installment in
USA TODAY *bestselling author Judy Duarte's*
new miniseries Rancho Esperanza.

On sale March 2021
Available wherever Harlequin books
and ebooks are sold.

**WE HOPE YOU ENJOYED
THIS BOOK FROM**

**HARLEQUIN
SPECIAL
EDITION**

Believe in love. Overcome obstacles. Find happiness.

Relate to finding comfort and strength in the
support of loved ones and enjoy the journey
no matter what life throws your way.

6 NEW BOOKS AVAILABLE EVERY MONTH!

COMING NEXT MONTH FROM

⊞ HARLEQUIN

SPECIAL EDITION

Available February 23, 2021

#2821 HIS SECRET STARLIGHT BABY
Welcome to Starlight • by Michelle Major
Former professional football player Jordan Shaeffer's game plan was simple: retire from football and set up a quiet life in Starlight. Then Cory Hall arrives with their infant and finds herself agreeing to be his fake fiancée until they work out a coparenting plan. Jordan may have rewritten the dating playbook...but will it be enough to bring this team together?

#2822 AN UNEXPECTED FATHER
The Fortunes of Texas: The Hotel Fortune • by Marie Ferrarella
Reformed playboy Brady Fortune has suddenly become guardian to his late best friend's little boys, and he's in *way* over his head! Then Harper Radcliffe comes to the rescue. The new nanny makes everything better, but now Brady is head over heels! Can Harper move beyond her past—and help Brady build a real family?

#2823 HIS FOREVER TEXAS ROSE
Men of the West • by Stella Bagwell
Trey Lasseter's instant attraction to the animal clinic's new receptionist spells trouble. But Nicole Nelson isn't giving up on her fresh start in this Arizona small town—or the hunky veterinary assistant. They could share so much more than a mutual affection for animals—and one dog in particular—if only Trey was ready to commit to the woman he's already fallen for!

#2824 MAKING ROOM FOR THE RANCHER
Twin Kings Ranch • by Christy Jeffries
To Dahlia King, Connor Remington is just another wannabe cowboy who'll go back to the city by midwinter. But underneath that city-slicker shine is a dedicated horseman who's already won the heart of Dahlia's animal-loving little daughter. But when her ex returns, Connor must decide to step up with this family...or step out.

#2825 SHE DREAMED OF A COWBOY
The Brands of Montana • by Joanna Sims
Cancer survivor Skyler Sinclair might live in New York City, but she's always dreamed of life on a Montana ranch. And at least part of that fantasy was inspired by her teenage crush on reality TV cowboy Hunter Brand. The more he gets to know the spirited Skyler, the more he realizes that he needs her more than she could ever need him...

#2826 THEIR NIGHT TO REMEMBER
Rancho Esperanza • by Judy Duarte
Thanks to one unforgettable night with a stranger, Alana Perez's dreams of motherhood are coming true! But when Clay Hastings literally stumbles onto her ranch with amnesia, he remembers nothing of the alluring cowgirl. Under her care, though, Clay begins to remember who he is...and the real reason he went searching for Alana...

YOU CAN FIND MORE INFORMATION ON UPCOMING HARLEQUIN TITLES, FREE EXCERPTS AND MORE AT HARLEQUIN.COM.

HSECNM0221

"We need to get our story straight," she reminded him.

His smile faded. "It's best not to offer too many details. We met in Atlanta, and now we have Ben."

She turned to face him, adjusting the lap belt as she shifted. "Your family's not going to question you showing up with a six-month-old baby? Like maybe you would have mentioned it to them prior to now?"

One bulky shoulder lifted and lowered. "I told you we aren't close."

"Your mom not knowing she has a grandchild is a bit more than 'not close,'" Cory felt compelled to point out. "Will she be upset we aren't married?"

"I'm not sure."

Her stomach tightened at his response. "Will she want to have a relationship with Ben after this weekend?"

"Good question."

"I have a million of them where that came from," she said. "I don't even know how your father died."

"Heart attack."

"Sudden." She worried her lower lip between her teeth. There were so many potential potholes for her to tumble into this weekend, and based on the tight set of his jaw, Jordan was in no shape to help navigate her through it. In fact, she had the feeling she'd be the one supporting him and he'd need solace well beyond a distraction.

"Can you answer a question with more than two words?" She was careful to make her voice light and was rewarded when his posture gentled somewhat.

"I suppose so."

"A bonus word. Nice. I'm sorry about your father's death," she said, giving in to the urge to reach out and place her hand on his arm.

Don't miss
His Secret Starlight Baby *by Michelle Major,*
available March 2021 wherever
Harlequin Special Edition books and ebooks are sold.

Harlequin.com